SURGEON IN DISGRACE

A martinet and a sourpuss — that's Sister Sarah Sweet's reputation at Hartlake, where she runs Women's Surgical with an iron hand. Her resentful staff do not suspect that handsome surgeon Patrick Egan is the cause for her unhappiness, for although Sarah obviously dislikes him he's never done anything to offend her — or has he? The tougher Sister Sweet gets, the more Mr Egan begins to remember a hazy incident in the past . . .

LYNNE COLLINS

SURGEON IN DISGRACE

Complete and Unabridged

LINFORD
Leicester

First published in Great Britain

First Linford Edition
published 1998

British Library CIP Data

Collins, Lynne, 1933–
    Surgeon in disgrace.—Large print ed.—
Linford romance library
    1. Love stories
    2. Large type books
    I. Title
    823.9'14 [F]

    ISBN 0-7089-5304-2

Published by
F. A. Thorpe (Publishing) Ltd.
Anstey, Leicestershire

Set by Words & Graphics Ltd.
Anstey, Leicestershire
Printed and bound in Great Britain by
T. J. International Ltd., Padstow, Cornwall

This book is printed on acid-free paper

1

Tall and slender in the dark blue frock, the distinctive organza cap set firmly on the shining coil of her dark hair, the slight severity of her expression at odds with the loveliness of delicately sculptured features, Sister Sarah Sweet passed through the heavy glass doors into the bustling Main Hall to begin another day on duty at Hartlake Hospital.

Jimmy, the head porter, turned from slotting a senior registrar's name board into position to show that he was on duty. His round red face broke into a smile of approval as she passed the desk. 'Good morning, Sister . . .'

He'd known Sarah Sweet since her early training days and he'd tipped her then as a sure bet for a ward sister's job one day. If she wasn't snapped up by a young doctor in search of a

1

wife from among the rank of Hartlake nurses, he'd thought shrewdly.

But few young doctors had marriage in mind when they pursued the nurses. They seldom had the time or the money for serious involvement during their long years of training. Flirtation was rife, however, despite Matron's vigilance and the hospital rules. The traditional uniform of a Hartlake nurse seemed to give even the plainest girl an appealing air of feminine prettiness.

Priding himself on knowing almost everything about almost every member of the staff, Jimmy knew that Sister Sweet had never encouraged the pursuit of the young doctors and medical students even in her first-year days. She'd always been slightly shy, rather reserved and reticent about her personal affairs. It puzzled him that such an attractive young woman apparently lacked a succession of boyfriends, and he often commented on it to his cronies among the porters.

Sarah smiled at him, quick and

warm, and walked on to the lifts. Jimmy was a hospital institution. Like the Barbary Apes, a medical student had once quipped. It was said that if the apes ever left the Rock, Gibraltar would crumble. If Jimmy ever left Hartlake, the hospital foundations would surely be threatened, for he *was* Hartlake to many of the regular patients who had passed through its portals in the last thirty years.

The lift carried Sarah up to the third floor and Mallory, Women's Surgical. As always, her pulses quickened and the adrenalin began to flow as she walked along the wide corridor to her ward, for she loved her work with all its interest and satisfaction.

It had taken a few weeks to adjust to the rapid turnover of patients and the faster pace of a surgical ward after being in charge of Fleming, Men's Medical, for so many months. But she had been flattered by Matron's confidence in her ability and efficiency, and no one had been allowed to suspect that she wasn't as confident as she seemed when she took over the reins. Now, she was enjoying the sense of urgency, the variety of cases, the daily demands and the constant challenge of the new job.

'Good morning, Sister . . . '

She paused to speak to the elderly woman patient who was making her slow and painful way to the bathrooms, clutching towel and sponge bag. 'Good morning, Mrs Foster. You're doing very well,' she approved. 'You'll be running along the corridor by the end of the week!'

'Running home, I hope, love!'

Sarah smiled. 'Well, that's possible. I know Doctor is very pleased with you.' Her smile and voice as she spoke the few words of praise and reassurance held a warmth and a sweetness that the junior nurses seldom saw and heard.

She knew she was better liked by the patients than by her team of nurses, but she was determined to run Mallory with the same degree of discipline and observance of etiquette that had already earned her the nick-name of Sister Sour among the juniors. She took her work seriously and it annoyed her that some girls seemed to look on nursing as just another job, resenting rules and regulations and the routine of ward work and the necessary authority of senior staff.

Sarah believed that nursing was a vocation and that any follower in Florence Nightingale's footsteps should embrace the long hours, the never-ending rounds and the hard work with a real desire to care for the sick and disabled and dying. So she had little time for any nurse who wasn't prepared to work until she dropped if the needs of the patients should demand it of her. For her part, she worked just as hard as any junior on the ward and was always ready to roll up her sleeves and help out with any chore, however menial, when they were particularly busy.

'Good morning, Sister . . .'

Audrey Crane, Senior Staff Nurse, greeted her with an audible sigh of relief as she entered the office with its panoramic window that overlooked the ward.

'Good morning, Staff. Had a bad night?' As Sarah made her way to the office, the keen glance that swept the ward where the nurses were busy with the last of the morning routines before going off duty had observed several neglected chores. Now she noticed the rather grubby apron that the staff nurse wore, the weariness stamped on her face and the strands of pale blonde hair that straggled from the loose knot on her neck. She didn't comment, but the slight frown in the sapphire eyes spoke volumes.

No matter how rushed she might be during the busy day, Sarah took pains to appear neat and clean and unruffled at all times, for she felt that patients quickly lost confidence in a nurse who was untidy and obviously harassed.

'I think one could say that without fear of contradiction,' Audrey said dryly, slightly on the defensive as she felt the unspoken criticism in the senior nurse's glance. 'Mrs Warren haemorrhaged and had to be rushed to Theatres. Mrs Lowe died. Miss Lorimer pulled out her stomach tube and Dr Hardy had to be called out of bed in the middle of the night to put it back, which didn't please him. And we had two emergency admissions. An acute appendicitis and a perforated ulcer, both listed for immediate surgery.'

Sarah nodded. 'Quite a night,' she agreed. 'I dare say you've entered full details in your report?'

'Yes, Sister.' It was demurely said, but the staff nurse's eyes sparked with resentment. Sarah Sweet imagined that no one but herself knew about efficiency, she thought crossly. Yet she'd been running Mallory at night for some weeks before the new broom arrived from Fleming, complete with the reputation she'd already earned as a martinet and a sourpuss.

The report was pushed across the desk

and Sarah bent her dark head to glance at it briefly, aware of undercurrents. 'It's a marvel of neatness considering how little time you must have had to write it up,' she said, smoothing feathers that she'd unintentionally ruffled.

The tired nurse was mollified. A word of praise from the austere ward sister was a rare event. 'I don't think I've forgotten to note anything, Sister.'

'I'm sure you haven't.' Sarah smiled and closed the book. 'We'll go through it when the day staff come on duty . . . ' She knew that Audrey Crane was thorough and reliable and a very good nurse. She also knew that she was still smarting because the plum post of Sister on Mallory had gone to another ward sister instead of to herself, as she'd hoped. Sympathising with a very natural disappointment, Sarah was ready to make allowances for a faint hostility in the staff nurse's attitude during the brief period when their duties overlapped.

They didn't know each other well.

They were both Hartlake-trained but from different sets, and there were so many wards and departments to the famous teaching hospital that two nurses could work within its walls for a very long time without meeting, on or off duty.

Besides, once a nurse reached the dizzy heights of ward sister, her 'strings' seemed to set her apart from her fellow nurses and few of them attempted to bridge the gulf unless they were already her friends.

Sarah had discovered during the first days on Fleming that a ward sister spent her days on a lonely pinnacle for the most part. She prided herself on being too self-sufficient to mind, but there were times when she missed the fun and the fellowship of early training days. Sadly, most of her set were no longer at Hartlake.

She hung up her cloak in the cupboard and put on the pristine white apron that was the symbol of being on duty for every nurse. She fastened the wide black belt about a very slender waist, silver clasp gleaming, and securely pinned the silver fob watch and small silver Hartlake badge to the bib of the apron. Then she turned back to the staff nurse, still seated behind the big desk.

'Your nurses seem to be a little behind with their work this morning, Staff. I think we could give them a hand, don't you?'

Audrey rose reluctantly. She felt that she'd earned ten minutes with her feet up in the comparative peace of the ward office while the juniors scurried to finish their routines. She knew better than to say so to Sarah Sweet, who was already rolling up her sleeves and slipping on frilled organza cuffs in readiness to help with bed-making and washing.

'Yes, of course, Sister,' she agreed dutifully, stifling a sigh and easing aching feet in the low-heeled black brogues.

A chorus of 'good mornings' greeted

Sarah as she made her way along the ward. She smiled at each patient in turn as she walked between the double row of beds with their neatly-spaced lockers and cheerfully bright curtains. The staff nurse followed in her wake, trying not to look as though it had been a very long night and she was virtually dead on her feet.

Sarah's first duty was to acquaint herself with the new admissions, and so she went directly to the bedside of the seventeen-year-old schoolgirl admitted during the night with abdominal pain and listed for an appendicectomy that morning. The patient was curled in the foetal position with the covers pulled firmly over her head.

'She's had her pre-med, Sister,' Audrey said in reply to an enquiring lift of an eyebrow. 'We're just waiting for Theatres to ring down to say that they're ready to receive her. She's the first on Mr Egan's list and he's coming to see her before she goes to Theatres.'

Sarah nodded. Then she put a gentle hand on the girl's shoulder. 'Beverley . . . ' A wan face emerged from the huddle of bedclothes, revealing that the patient was very young and very apprehensive. 'Good morning, dear. I'm Sister,' she said with the swift, sweet smile that the patients found so reassuring and the warmth of concern in her dark blue eyes. 'Nurse tells me that you came in during the night. How are you this morning?'

'Feeling rotten . . . '

'I know you can't be very comfortable just now,' Sarah sympathised. 'But we shall be doing something about that very soon. I expect Nurse Crane has explained things to you?'

'Yes. Going to take out my appendix, she said.'

'That's right. You've had an injection that's making you rather sleepy, I know. Soon you'll be going with one of the nurses to the operating theatre and then you'll have another injection to send you off to sleep. When you wake up, you'll be back in the ward and feeling much better. There's absolutely no reason for you to be anxious about anything, Beverley. You'll soon be perfectly well again.'

'When will I be able to go home, Sister?'

'Oh, in about four or five days, I expect.'

The girl visibly brightened. 'That soon?'

'Probably.' Sarah mentally crossed her fingers to ward off the possibility of complications. But the patient was young and healthy and there was nothing on her chart to indicate that she shouldn't make a rapid recovery from a routine appendicectomy.

'What about school, Sister? How long before I can go back to school? I'm taking A-levels next month.' The pre-med was taking effect and the words were slightly slurred.

'Your own doctor will advise you about that. But we usually recommend three to four weeks' convalescence. So you'll have plenty of time for studying for the exams.'

Beverley managed a wan smile. 'I guess I didn't time it right, Sister. It's another five weeks!'

Sarah laughed and patted her hand. 'I'm sure you'll sail through them,' she declared and moved away to talk to the other new patient.

Mrs Lomax was a business-woman who ran several boutiques and had been too busy to heed the warning symptoms of a stomach ulcer. Irregular meals, too much alcohol and too many cigarettes, combined with the stress of competing in a very commercial world, had eventually caused the perforation of her ulcer. Now, listed for a laparotomy and repair, she was in some pain despite medication. Rather grey-faced, she complained of nausea and headache as well as stomach pain, her manicured hands continually fretting at the sheets.

'All these doctors coming and going with their questions and their tests and their blood samples, and no one really does a thing to make me feel any better,' she said querulously.

'You'll be going to the theatre very soon, Mrs Lomax. But there are routine procedures to be followed before we can operate,' Sarah said firmly. The duty houseman had set up an intravenous infusion and she checked the position of the cannula and the flow of the drip while she explained that the patient's discomfort was possibly caused to some extent by the antibiotics that the doctor had prescribed to combat any post-operative complications. 'Unfortunately, there are one or two minor side-effects to this particular drug, but they are short-lived.'

Mrs Lomax looked sceptical. 'My throat hurts,' she said huskily. 'That young doctor was very clumsy and scraped it badly when he put down this awful tube. It's so uncomfortable, Sister. Must I have it?'

Sarah checked the nasogastric tube

and aspirator that Dr Hardy had inserted in readiness for post-operative care of the patient. He might have been a little rushed but he was a very capable doctor, and she suspected that it was the woman's lack of co-operation that had caused a minor scraping of the throat.

'There is a slight abrasion,' she agreed. 'But that will heal quickly. I'm afraid you must have the tube, Mrs Lomax. For the time being. But I promise that we'll remove it as soon as possible after surgery. Now just try to relax, my dear. In a little while, Nurse will give you an injection that should make you feel much less anxious about everything . . .'

Well used to all kinds of patients, Sarah could recognise a potentially difficult one in Mrs Lomax, who was already fretting about the enforced absence from her busy office. Nothing would be right for that one in the days to come, she suspected, moving away from the bed. Within a day or two she

16

could be feeling well enough to demand a bed in a side ward so that she could deal with her business affairs in peace and privacy and monopolise the trolley telephone.

Obviously sharing her thoughts, Audrey Crane raised a meaningful eyebrow as they walked along the ward. 'Trouble with a capital T,' she murmured meaningfully.

'Possibly. But she won't have much to say for herself for the first few days and I shall have her measure by the time she feels up to being troublesome,' Sarah said briskly.

The staff nurse had no reason to doubt the coolly confident words. No patient was allowed to be difficult or disruptive on Sarah Sweet's ward, she thought dryly, while admitting that her colleague had a way with patients that was very effective.

She could quell the liveliest junior with a glance or shrivel a bumptious houseman with a word, too. And she didn't hesitate to challenge even the crustiest of consultants if she didn't agree with a suggested treatment for one of her precious patients.

She was a stern disciplinarian and not at all popular with the juniors, who complained that she had no heart and very little patience and sent them to Matron for the least thing. Even allowing for exaggeration, it seemed that Sister Sweet was bent on living up to her nickname of Sister Sour. Yet the patients loved her, declaring that she was all heart and understanding, so kind and thoughtful and always willing to do what she could to ensure their comfort and welfare and peace of mind.

An enigma, Audrey decided, as they made beds together while the day staff gradually filtered into the ward and hurried to help the night nurses at a meaningful nod from the ward sister. A dual personality. A mystery woman who never talked about herself and didn't endear herself to her fellow nurses with that air of chilly reserve.

She was a good-looking girl with that profusion of rich dark hair, the sparkling dark blue eyes, classic features and a slender and very shapely figure, Audrey admitted. As one of the prettiest nurses at Hartlake who never lacked for admirers, she could afford to be generous. Men noticed Sarah Sweet, of course. But she seemed to be too dedicated to nursing to have the time or the inclination to notice them. The grapevine never gossiped about Sister Sweet, although it could be busy enough with everyone else's affairs, Audrey thought dryly and rather ruefully.

Soon only one bed remained to be made. Between them, Sister and Staff Nurse helped the post-operative Mrs Nicholls into a chair. She was a jolly woman with a glandular problem that affected her weight so that she was several stone heavier than she should be, and it took both slightly-built nurses to transfer her from bed to chair with the apparently effortless ease that came from years of training and practical experience.

'It don't seem right that bits of girls like you should have to struggle with a great lump of lard like me,' Mrs Nicholls declared, doing her best to help herself, panting with the exertion and wincing as the stitches of a recent cholecystectomy pulled at her tender flesh. 'Could do yourselves a lot of damage, lifting heavy weights, you know!'

'Oh, we're used to it, Mrs Nicholls.' Sarah exchanged an amused glance with the staff nurse, who shared her appreciation at being referred to as 'bits of girls' when they were both well into their twenties and matured by several years of nursing. 'We're trained to lift patients without hurting them or ourselves.'

'Well, you makes it seem easy, I must say. But it still don't seem right,' she persisted, flushed and breathless and sweating profusely.

Sarah paused in the act of straightening

the sheet to pat her plump hand. 'It's very sweet of you to worry about us, Mrs Nicholls,' she said warmly. 'But we're all much tougher than we look.'

Nurses had to be, she amended silently. They soon fell by the wayside if they couldn't keep up with the many demands that were made on their energy and their enthusiasm for the job.

'It's a man's job, lifting. That's what I think, Sister. What about him, for instance?' Mrs Nicholls jerked her greying head at the tall man in the long white coat who had just pushed through the swing doors of the ward. 'He's got a pair of shoulders on him!'

'That's Mr Egan.' The staff nurse spoke quickly, shocked. 'He's one of our senior surgeons, Mrs Nicholls. I don't think he'd take kindly to the job of hospital porter!'

'Bit of a snob, is he? That's a shame, then. I wouldn't mind being manhandled by one like that. Tall, dark and *very* handsome! How about you, Sister?' Mrs Nicholls winked at Sarah in outrageous implication, her whole frame shaking as she chuckled.

Sarah didn't smile. 'I'm sure that Mr Egan would be happy to oblige, but we can manage very well without him,' she said lightly, slightly cool. 'Ready, Staff . . . ?'

She didn't even glance towards the tall surgeon, too intent on getting her patient back into bed. He waited, dutifully observing the ward etiquette that didn't allow him to examine a patient without permission from Sister or the senior nurse in charge, but conveying just a hint of impatience with his frequent glances along the ward.

He *did* have a pair of shoulders on him, Sarah thought, dryly echoing the patient's approval. In his medical student days, Patrick Egan had been a very useful member of the Hartlake rugger team. Sarah had known him in those days. Once, she'd known him rather too well — and she had very good cause to remember and regret.

He'd obviously forgotten a brief and meaningless interlude with a first-year nurse met at a wild student party. But there were some things that a girl could never forget. Or forgive.

He *was* tall, dark and very handsome, but these days she was entirely immune to the striking good looks and the physical magnetism that caused such havoc among the junior nurses. Once she'd been an impressionable and susceptible junior, sighing over the attractive surgeon, but it was a long time since her heart had foolishly bumped in her breast for the mere sight of Patrick Egan as he walked into a ward where she was working or strode along a hospital corridor ahead of her or talked to a colleague in Main Hall as she passed through it on her way on or off duty. She had learned the hard way that he was not to be trusted . . .

Mrs Nicholls was soon comfortably settled against the banked pillows, complete with trailing drainage tube that led to a plastic container beneath the bed. The two nurses turned away from a final exchange of light-hearted banter with the cheerful and good-natured patient.

Sarah glanced at the surgeon who stood with hands thrust deep into the pockets of his white coat, regarding the ward with a slight glower of impatience.

'Get the day staff together for Report, please, Staff. As soon as that's done, you can go off duty at long last. I'll just have a word with Mr Egan,' she said briskly.

But she didn't hurry to his side for she paused once or twice to speak to a patient as she made her way down the ward ....

2

A frown lurked in the surgeon's deep-set dark eyes as she made her leisurely way along the ward towards him. Reaching him, the smile that she had bestowed with such warmth and sweetness on the patients faded swiftly from her lips and eyes. 'Mr Egan . . . ' She greeted him coolly, formally, without any hint of welcome.

'Good morning, Sister.' He was due in Theatre and there was a snap of impatience in the deep voice, as though he suspected her of deliberately keeping him waiting.

As she had, Sarah admitted, unrepentant. 'What can I do for you, Mr Egan?'

'I've a patient on your ward. Beverley James. Dr Hardy admitted her during the night and she's on my list for an appendicectomy.' He wasted no time on pleasantries for a ward sister who disliked and disapproved of him and made it obvious. Her attitude didn't bother him unduly. It seemed to him that Sarah Sweet liked very few of his colleagues. She ran the ward efficiently and looked after his patients to his satisfaction and that suited him.

'Yes, that's right. She's in bed twelve . . . '

As Sarah spoke, the ward doors swung back to admit two hurrying, white-coated doctors. The surgeon turned to regard them with a sardonic lift to an eyebrow.

'Managed to find your way at last, I see,' he said dryly, his tone rebuking their late arrival. He brushed aside a murmur of apology with an impatient, slightly arrogant wave of the hand. 'Sister, I don't know if you've met the new members of Sir Lionel's team? Jeff Wyman, Junior Registrar. Harriet Blake, Senior House Officer.'

Sarah acknowledged the introduction with a nod and a smile for each in turn.

'How do you do? We shall be seeing a lot of each other, so I hope you've been warned that I'm an old-fashioned ward sister and that you won't get away with any irregularities,' she said lightly, but briskly purposeful.

Harriet Blake smiled. 'Such as flirting with your nurses?' she drawled. 'That won't be a problem where I'm concerned, of course. I can't speak for Mr Wyman.' It was smooth, slightly amused, very self-possessed.

Sarah observed the elegant femininity despite the classic tailoring of her grey flannel skirt and grey silk shirt, the severity of the clinical white coat. Ash-blonde hair was expertly cut in a short thick fall, framing a heart-shaped face, and fashionably large horn-rimmed glasses magnified lovely amber eyes that regarded her with such cool confidence that she felt an instant and unreasonable dislike of the woman.

'Inexperienced doctors are usually guilty of worse faults,' she said crisply, putting Harriet Blake firmly in her place.

Jeff Wyman chuckled. Meeting humorous grey eyes in a lean, intelligent face, Sarah was disarmed by the warm and friendly understanding and a hint of admiration in their depths.

Experience had taught her to be wary of all men, but she found herself rather liking this one on sight, quite unexpectedly. A smile flickered briefly, rewarding him. Then, oddly and unusually flustered, she turned back to the unsmiling Patrick Egan.

'Bed Twelve,' she repeated coolly. 'Will you need me? Nurse Crane is waiting to make the report before she goes off duty.'

'No, I don't think so, thanks. The patient has had her pre-med, I suppose?' The dark eyes had seen more than she suspected or he meant to betray by the indifference of his tone and expression. But the surgeon was slightly surprised and instantly intrigued to discover a glimpse of

NB

warm and feminine humanity beneath the starch.

'Half an hour ago.'

He nodded. 'Very well. Thank you, Sister.' He turned away and the new house officer fell into step at his side, her cool voice carrying as she put a pertinent question about the patient to him.

The auburn-headed registrar made no immediate move to follow them. Sarah glanced at him with a query in her sapphire eyes and he grinned at her.

'I hope you meant it when you said that we'd be seeing a lot of each other, Sister,' he said lightly, grey eyes twinkling.

She was surprised into a smile. 'On the ward, Mr Wyman,' she said, mock stern. 'And you'll probably see more of me than you wish. My nurse will tell you that there's no escape from my eagle eye or my sharp tongue — and I make no allowances for rank!'

Jeff shook his head. 'I can't believe

that you're really such a dragon. You're much too lovely,' he said simply. There was an unmistakable interest and admiration in the way he looked and smiled and spoke.

The colour flew into Sarah's face at the totally unexpected words. But she only laughed, knowing that amusement was a very useful method of countering such approaches.

'Don't break any rules on my ward or you'll find that I really *do* breathe fire, Mr Wyman — and the first rule to remember is that you mustn't try to flirt with me,' she said coolly.

She walked away from him, starched skirts rustling, hoping that she'd sounded friendly but firm. He had charm and an easy manner that she liked, but she didn't mean to encourage his obvious interest. Many doctors enjoyed a brief relaxation from the demands of their work in a little light-hearted flirtation. It might be meaningless and harmless but it was still frowned on by Matron and therefore avoided by any sensible nurse. At least while she was on duty.

Sarah owed her much-prized 'strings' to being sensible and hard-working and dedicated for a number of years. Since that brief and utterly disastrous involvement with Patrick Egan in her first year of training, she'd successfully kept every man at a safe distance.

So it was disconcerting to realise that she'd warmed in unexpected and rather foolish fashion to the friendly overtures of a complete stranger . . .

★ ★ ★

Grouped about the desk in the ward office, the day staff listened and made careful notes while Audrey Crane rattled off details of the new admissions, current condition of previous patients and any treatment that had been necessary during the night.

Sarah's attention wandered slightly as Patrick Egan and his colleagues passed the open door on their way from the ward. The surgeon hadn't spent long with his young patient. The case promised to be a straightforward appendicectomy and he'd merely made a routine check before surgery.

She'd heard him say that his new assistant could remove the girl's appendix, and Sarah found herself hoping that the likeable registrar would acquit himself well enough to satisfy a man who was known to be a clever, conscientious and caring surgeon who demanded the very best from everyone who worked with him.

Patrick Egan had qualified at Hartlake and walked the wards for the stipulated year before leaving to work in various hospitals to gain experience and work for his Fellowship. Three months ago he'd returned to Hartlake as Sir Lionel Fielding's senior registrar, much to Sarah's dismay. Out of sight hadn't been entirely out of mind, but at least she'd been spared constant reminders of something that she was taking too long to forget, and she'd hoped never to see him again.

She'd accepted the job of ward sister on Mallory before she realised that it would bring her into almost daily contact with the surgeon. His work had never brought him to Fleming, a medical ward, since he'd come back to Hartlake, and she'd avoided any social occasions when they might have met.

Her first morning on the new ward had been tense and uncomfortable while she waited for him to arrive to do his round — and then she'd wondered dryly why she'd imagined that he might remember her out of the many women he must have known since his medical student days. Hadn't she sometimes wondered if he'd even known her name on a night that had been so memorable for her but obviously of little importance to him?

On that first morning Patrick Egan had been courteous and charming and complimentary about Mallory's gain and Fleming's loss. But there'd been no flicker of recognition or real interest. Totally unmoved by the smile in the dark eyes and the pleasant warmth of the deep voice, Sarah had been cool and brisk and efficient. In the days that followed, he'd taken his cue from the slightly starchy manner that kept him firmly at a distance. Now he was always impersonal and as cool as herself, and wasted few words on her even when they discussed one of his patients.

Sarah frequently wished that circumstances hadn't brought him back to Hartlake, but she had no intention of allowing his unexpected and unwelcome return to drive her from the hospital that had become her second home and almost her entire life . . .

Audrey Crane finished Report in a sudden rush and hurried away. Sarah delegated various jobs to her nurses and then went to check the contents of the drugs trolley before she began the medicine round.

The night staff nurse was talking to Patrick Egan in the corridor, and Sarah wondered if the girl had rushed out of the office to catch the surgeon before he left the ward. There was no sign of the red-headed registrar or the blonde and beautiful Harriet Blake.

It seemed to be a very intimate exchange between surgeon and staff nurse, although Sarah was too far away to hear any of it and had no desire to eavesdrop. She crossed the corridor to the clinical room, carefully not glancing in their direction, searching for the key to the drugs trolley on the bunch that Audrey had handed to her before going off duty.

It was inevitable that she should overhear some of the gossip that was bandied about between the juniors in the ward kitchen or sluice when they ought to be getting on with their work. So Sarah knew that Patrick Egan was rumoured to be dating the staff nurse on a fairly regular basis and that the grapevine had actually hinted at the possibility of an engagement in the near future.

He was a very attractive man, so it wasn't at all surprising that the juniors gossiped about him and sometimes cast out lures in his direction. He was a sensual man, too, as Sarah knew to her cost. There had obviously been several women in his life, although he wasn't so much a rake as a determined bachelor, she thought dryly, counting capsules and tablets and checking the levels of various bottles.

He was a dedicated, ambitious man, too. Knowing that he was working towards a consultancy, Sarah thought it unlikely that he had marriage in mind at this stage in his career. He wasn't the kind of man to be swayed by sentiment, she felt. But it seemed that Audrey Crane was hoping to succeed where other women had failed, and she wished her luck with a scornful shrug of her slim shoulders. The staff nurse was welcome to a man who had neither heart nor conscience, judging by his behaviour in the past, she thought with a familiar stirring of contempt.

'Can you spare a moment, Sister?'

Sarah glanced over her shoulder at

the sound of the surgeon's deep and slightly peremptory voice. 'Yes. What is it, Mr Egan?' Her tone implied that he'd chosen an inconvenient moment.

'I believe we agreed that Mrs Hartley might go home today. I'm going to be busy in Theatres for most of the morning, so perhaps I ought to sign the discharge certificate while I'm on the ward?'

'Yes, of course . . . ' Sarah closed and locked the trolley and slipped the keys into the pocket of her dark blue frock. Then she turned to him. 'If you'll just come along to the office.'

Her quiet voice was tinged with its usual frost, and Patrick wondered dryly how and when he'd given her cause for such obvious dislike.

At the very back of his mind was an elusive memory of something to do with this girl. He knew she was Hartlake-trained. Maybe he'd met her at some time during his wild student days when he'd worked his amorous and unthinking way through a number of junior nurses. But Sarah Sweet hadn't been one of his conquests. He wouldn't have forgotten her so completely. Besides, his weakness was for pretty blondes rather than attractive brunettes, he reminded himself.

She was a good-looking girl, but sharp-tongued and critical — and apparently her nickname of Sister Sour was well-deserved. His colleagues declared that she was an iceberg.

But she'd softened at a smile from the new registrar that morning, so maybe she wasn't as frigid as she seemed. Patrick had no real interest in finding out for himself, but his dark eyes rested with male appreciation on the neat waist and slim hips and the thrust of tilting breasts beneath the bib of her apron as she came out of the clinical room. And he noted the slender and very shapely legs as he followed her along the corridor to the office.

As they entered, the telephone shrilled. Sarah reached for it automatically. 'Mallory — Sister speaking . . . ' It was one of the theatre sisters and she listened to the familiar, disembodied voice of a friend without any change of expression. Then she said, 'Yes, I'll tell him. Thank you, Sister.' She put down the receiver. 'The porters are on their way to collect your appendicectomy patient, Mr Egan.'

She didn't tell him that Liz had laughingly demanded to know why he was still on Mallory when he ought to be scrubbed up and donning mask and gown and gloves in readiness to operate on his patient. She didn't tell him that Liz had scolded her for keeping the man from his work, a teasing lilt to the warm voice. Even Liz, a close friend since training days, didn't know that Patrick Egan was the last man in the world that she would wish to detain with flirtation in mind, even if he was inclined to indulge her. It added insult to injury that she was not really his type and never had been.

'Oh, I've decided to let Wyman do that one,' he said carelessly. 'It will give

39

me a chance to observe his technique and see if he's as good as he's supposed to be. Friend of yours, by the way, Sister?'

'No. Why do you ask?' Sarah was slightly on the defensive, despite the casualness of the question, wondering if he'd sensed her absurd and unexpected response to the charm of a total stranger.

The surgeon shrugged. 'No reason. It was just an impression that you already knew each other.'

Sarah shook her head, reached for a discharge certificate and pushed it across the desk towards him for signature, together with her own slim gold pen. 'I'll fill in the patient's details later,' she said briskly, watching as he signed his name on the form. 'I know that you're in a hurry . . . '

'Meaning that *you* are . . . ' Straightening, Patrick glanced at her with a slight smile quirking the warmly sensual mouth, perversely inclined to linger just because she so obviously

40

wanted him to leave. 'Anxious to get on with your work or just anxious to be rid of me, Sister? Don't you trust me around your first-years?' The humorous words mocked the grapevine gossip and invited her to share his indulgent amusement at the silliness of juniors who exaggerated a smile or a few light words into a non-existent interest.

Sarah didn't trust that unexpected lowering of a reserve that had matched her own cool impersonality for weeks. For some reason, he seemed to be trying to charm her into liking him — but he wouldn't succeed.

She smiled frostily, unamused. 'I imagine that you must have outgrown your tendency to run amok with first-year nurses, Mr Egan.'

Patrick raised an eyebrow, immediately intrigued by a slight barb in her tone. 'That sounds as if you knew me in former days,' he drawled. 'Before I left Hartlake for pastures new and became a reformed character . . . ' She said nothing. He studied the set but rather lovely face with new interest. 'Knew me and disapproved of me? Is that it?' There was a hint of mockery in the deep voice. 'What are you, Sister? Twenty-four, twenty-five? Not much more, surely? You must have been a first-year during my stint as med student or houseman. How is it that I missed you, I wonder? You're an attractive girl.'

Sarah picked up the signed certificate and placed it carefully in the patient's folder, trying not to let him see that her hands were trembling with suppressed anger. 'It's time for the medicine round, Mr Egan. My staff nurse will be waiting. So if you'll excuse me . . . '

'Maybe I *didn't* miss you?' he said abruptly as if she hadn't spoken, sensitive to her sudden tension and observing the spark of annoyance in the lovely sapphire eyes. 'You obviously don't like me. You must have a reason. Did I make a pass and get my face slapped in those long-ago days?'

He saw the beginning of an angry flush in the delicate oval face, the tightening of the perfect mouth, and almost caught the tail of that elusive memory at the very back of his mind. He was suddenly sure that he was on the right track.

'If you can't remember then I'm surprised that you suppose *I* should,' Sarah said icily, taut with pride.

He shrugged. 'It happened too often.' His dark eyes gleamed with amused recollection of those wild student days. 'But I shouldn't think that men made passes at you very often . . . '

'Unless they were drunk at the time?' she suggested very sweetly, very bitter.

Patrick heard and thought he understood the anger and the resentment. 'That isn't what I meant. You're not very approachable,' he told her frankly, the warmth of his smile intended to take any sting from the words. 'Maybe you never were. Maybe you were always too much of a Florence Nightingale to have much time for men. The dedicated nurse with her nose in her books every night. The kind of student nurse who is more concerned with getting her badge than getting a husband. An increasingly rare species, I might add!'

Sarah refused to be softened by the charm of his smile or the engaging twinkle in the dark eyes. He would never disarm her again, she thought coldly.

'Any girl is better off with her books than getting involved with medical students with only one thing in mind,' she said tartly.

The impulsive words were angry and revealing. Patrick studied her thoughtfully. 'So you've nursed a grudge against me all these years, Sister? Rather unreasonable, don't you think?'

'Mr Egan, I have a great deal to do and I haven't the time or the inclination to discuss ancient history with you,' Sarah declared, pointedly looking at the small silver watch on her breast.

'Then we'll discuss it another time,' he suggested confidently. 'Over dinner one evening?'

'Over my dead body!'

He smiled. 'I can only try to make amends.'

'For an offence that you can't even remember committing?' She looked at him with icy contempt. 'Don't waste any more of my time, Mr Egan!'

Head high, back bristling with pride, she stalked from the office to vent a fraction of her fury with the surgeon on an unsuspecting nurse who chose the worst possible moment to drop a tray of newly-sterilised instruments as she took it from the autoclave.

Listening to a little of the tirade, Patrick understood just why she had been nicknamed Sister Sour by the juniors. He turned to walk along the corridor to the lift that would whisk him up to the theatre floor, wondering wryly if some of her sourness was really due to an offence that he couldn't remember committing.

It seemed so unlikely, even ridiculous. But first-year nurses were often very shy and very sensitive and sometimes totally inexperienced, and it seemed that he'd handled an amorous approach badly enough to have left a lasting impression on the young Sarah Sweet. It was damnable that he didn't have the slightest recollection of the incident — or the girl that she had been.

Surprisingly, he found that he was attracted by the woman that she had become despite the tartness of her tongue and the off-putting chill of her manner. He'd been serious about that dinner invitation — and not really surprised that she'd turned him down without the slightest hesitation.

She seemed to be a proud wench. He suspected that she could be passionate, too. Maybe it was the promise of fire beneath the ice that had originally caught his interest when she was a first-year and he was sowing his wild oats as a medical student . . .

'Excuse me, Sister . . . ' Helen

Champion, Senior Staff Nurse, interrupted the angry recital of the second-
year's recent sins, culminating in the
last straw that pointed in the direction
of Matron's office.

Sarah turned, still fuming. 'Well?
What is it, Staff? Surely you can
manage without me for just five
minutes?'

'Do you want me to begin the
medicine round, Sister? Nurse Scully
can help me.'

'No. I'm just coming. Thank you,
Staff.' She sent a final glare in
the direction of the bewildered and
chastened junior nurse. I'll leave you
to clear up this mess, Nurse Vincent
— and to think very carefully about
your future. There's no room in
nursing for someone as clumsy and
as careless as you seem to be. We can
do without dreamers at Hartlake, too!
Other hospitals may be less fussy!'

'Yes, Sister. I'm sorry, Sister . . . '
Three bags full, Sister, the girl muttered
rebelliously beneath her breath as she

stooped to pick up the scattered surgical instruments.

'That girl is a sore trial!' Sarah declared as Helen emerged from the clinical room with the drugs trolley. 'How on earth did she survive her first year?'

'She came to us from Accident and Emergency with a very good report.' Helen wondered what had shaken the ward sister's usual calm. She could be cold and stern and autocratic. She was seldom so passionate.

'Perhaps her disasters were more easily absorbed in the usual chaos of that department,' Sarah said, very dryly . . .

3

Sarah usually liked to take her time over the round, talking to the patients, assessing their progress or decline with an experienced eye, noting any particular problems or anxieties.

But that morning, feeling strangely unsettled and at odds with herself and everyone else, she whisked through it as quickly as possible and returned to the ward office to catch up on the pile of paperwork on her desk.

With a sheaf of forms in front of her, she reached for the slim gold pen that she always clipped to the inside of her apron bib. It was missing and she frowned. Then she remembered that Patrick Egan had used it to sign the discharge certificate for Mrs Hartley.

He hadn't returned it and it wasn't anywhere on her desk. Damn the man! He'd gone off with the pen — one that she valued because it had been a present from her parents when she achieved her state registration badge. But she was sure to see the surgeon some time during the day and she made a mental note to ask him for her pen . . .

Mrs Lomax was taken to Theatres half-way through the morning, still complaining despite the effects of the pre-med. Beverley James came down from the recovery room after surgery, accompanied by the new registrar who was still wearing the green theatre trousers and tunic and cap, green mask dangling by its tapes about his neck.

Sarah was teaching a first-year how to remove sutures when the little procession came into the ward. As soon as she could, she left the girl to carry on with the task, confident of her ability to do it properly. She was a very promising junior.

She whisked through the curtains that were drawn about the bed and dismissed the hovering nurse with a nod. 'Problems, Mr Wyman?'

'Not exactly. But it wasn't as straightforward as we expected, Sister.' Jeff Wyman bent over the girl, lifting an eyelid to examine the pupil. She had taken rather longer than he liked to come round from the anaesthetic and she had lapsed again into unconsciousness.

'The appendix was certainly inflamed, but the trouble was a diseased ovary. So we did both jobs . . . ovariectomy as well as the appendicectomy. She should be fine, of course.' The surgeon straightened, smiled. 'I'll keep a careful eye on her progress for a few days, however . . . and I shall want some special tests carried out.'

Sarah liked his decisive but courteous manner and she liked his concern, his personal involvement with the patient. She decided that he was going to be a valuable addition to Sir Lionel's team. She liked him, and for the first time in years she found herself warming to a man and wanting to know him better — and she felt that he meant to give

51

her the opportunity as she basked in the warmth of his smile.

She sent a nurse for the patient's folder so that he could make the necessary notes and listened carefully while he gave detailed verbal instructions for the immediate post-operative care of the schoolgirl. Then she walked with him to the swing doors of the ward.

'Going back to Theatres, Mr Wyman?' she asked lightly.

He nodded. 'Egan wants me to assist with a hernioplasty which seems to indicate that he considers my work to be up to standard. It's encouraging as I gather that he has the reputation of being hard to please.'

'He can be very critical and demanding. But he's a fair man and a very able surgeon.' Sarah was fair, too. She might not like Patrick Egan but she was ready to admit his ability and his skill as a surgeon.

'I expect you know him well, Sister.' It was tentative, almost probing.

'I've known him for some years,

of course,' she returned evasively. 'I trained here at Hartlake. So did he, as I expect you know.'

'Well, I'm a very new boy and feeling it,' he said smiling, his easy confidence belying the words. 'I need someone to show me the ropes.'

'I'm sure Mr Egan will be pleased to help in any way he can,' she told him demurely.

He threw her an amused and slightly reproachful glance. 'He seems a pleasant enough fellow. But women are so much more sympathetic,' he murmured meaningfully. 'Particularly nurses . . .'

'That's very true. But *ward sisters* are as hard as nails, Mr Wyman,' she told him firmly. But the beginning of a smile lurked in the dark blue eyes with their long sweep of black lashes.

'I'm Jeff to my friends,' he said promptly. 'And we *are* friends, I hope, Sarah.'

'I'm Sister Sweet while I'm on duty!'

He chuckled. 'Then we must meet

when you're off duty — and soon!' He pushed open the swing doors and paused. 'I'm giving a party for old and new friends tomorrow night, celebrating the new job. I hope you'll come along. Twenty Clifton Street, top floor flat. Bring the boyfriend if you like,' he added, gently probing.

Sarah went back to her work, the smile lingering in her eyes. She was rather tempted to go to his party although she usually avoided the Hartlake social scene. Few invitations came her way these days. She'd refused too many in the past and earned herself a reputation for being anti-social and stand-offish. Perhaps it was time to come out of her shell and prove that she could be just as friendly and forthcoming as other girls despite her 'strings'. Maybe she'd been wary of men for too long — and maybe she was overdue for a second look at love, she thought, almost defiantly.

Not that she'd ever been in love with Patrick Egan. Far from it. He'd merely been a first-year's fancy, admired from afar until that disastrous evening when she'd met him away from the hospital precincts for the first time and been foolishly flattered by the ardent attentions of an attractive young houseman who'd never appeared to notice her on the ward.

Knowing his reputation for casual affairs, she ought to have known better than to fall into his arms in return for a smile and a few meaningless words. But she'd had plenty of time for regrets — and very good cause, too. She might have been able to forgive herself for the folly of that night if she'd loved the man, she thought wryly.

She didn't mean to fall in love with the red-headed registrar either, for all his seeming niceness. Nursing was the most important thing in her life and she didn't want the complications of serious involvement with a man. Deep down, she just didn't trust any man any more.

But that didn't mean that she

couldn't enjoy the company of an attractive and likeable man if it was offered. So why not the one who had stirred her interest with his warm smile and twinkling grey eyes and lean good looks . . . ?

* * *

Sarah's long day on duty was usually relieved by a break during afternoon visiting when the patients neither needed nor wanted very much attention from the ward staff.

That afternoon she left Helen Champion in charge of the ward as usual. She was a good staff nurse. She had the right touch with the juniors and she was much more popular than herself, Sarah knew. But few ward sisters could expect to be liked if they were efficient and strict. It was more important that they should be respected and their instructions obeyed without question.

It wasn't so very long since her own

training days, and Sarah could recall the mingled awe and animosity with which she and her set had regarded the sisters and staff nurses who set them scurrying and constantly chivvied them through their chores. She felt much more sympathy for the first-years than she ever allowed them to know, in fact.

She was on her way from the ward when Patrick Egan stepped out of the lift and turned to walk along the corridor towards her. She paused, waiting for him, and he raised an enquiring eyebrow.

'My pen,' she said without preliminary, holding out her hand. 'You went off with it this morning. I'd like it back.'

There wasn't even the pretence of politeness or the least degree of friendliness in that chilly tone, and the surgeon's eyes narrowed in a slight frown.

'I was just on my way to return it to you, Sister. I found it lurking in the pocket of my coat when I changed in

Theatres, half an hour ago.'

His manner was pleasant enough, but something in his tone rebuked Sarah for an unnecessarily aggressive attitude. Or so she felt.

'Well, it didn't jump in there by itself,' she said tartly. She took the pen from him, unsmiling. 'Thank you . . . '

Deep-set dark eyes travelled over the slender figure, noting the significant absence of the white apron. 'Going off duty?'

'I'll be back at four. In the meantime, Nurse Champion is in charge of the ward and will attend to you, Mr Egan.'

Dismissing him with the brisk words, Sarah turned away and walked towards the lift. The surgeon fell into step at her side and she glanced at him in surprise.

'I'm off duty too, Sister. I only came to bring back your pen. I've left my patients in the apparently capable hands of my new colleague. How is the little girl on your ward, by the way?

58

That ovary was in very poor condition. Luckily the other one seemed to be fine, so she ought not to have any problems with eventual motherhood.'

'She's still rather comatose, but Mr Wyman is monitoring her carefully. He's already been to see her three times since she came down from Theatres.' In the lift, Sarah folded her arms across her breast in the traditional nurse's manner, drawing as far away from him as the confined space allowed, feeling uncomfortably aware of the potent physical magnetism that had been her downfall on a too-memorable occasion.

'Good man. He promises to be a very useful member of the team. Knows his job, cares about the patients and seems to know how to get on with people. What do you think of him, Sister?'

Sarah shrugged. 'Too soon to say,' she said briefly. She didn't mean to admit to an unexpected warmth of liking for the new registrar.

'What about the beautiful Harriet?'

The dark eyes were suddenly alive with merriment. 'Very sure of herself, isn't she? She talked her way into the job, but I wonder if she has the necessary stamina for surgery. Eight hours in an operating theatre can be very demanding and extremely tiring.'

'No job for a woman?' Sarah suggested very dryly.

He shook his dark head, smiling. 'You won't trap me with that one, Sister. I'm no chauvinist. And I've known some really good women surgeons.'

'Very few women opt for surgery, of course. But Miss Blake seems strong-minded enough to know what she's doing and what she wants.' Recalling the way that the blonde house officer had played up to the surgeon earlier that day, she suspected that Harriet Blake had already made up her mind to want Patrick Egan. The fur would fly if Audrey Crane suspected it too, she thought.

As the lift doors slid open, she

made her way through the people who crowded round to enter and began to cross Main Hall, hurrying to escape the darkly handsome surgeon. As far as she was concerned, it was the parting of the ways — and not a moment too soon!

Those few moments of descent from third floor to ground level had seemed an eternity to Sarah. Despising herself for the stirring of response to the man's masculinity, she hoped he hadn't sensed the turmoil of her thoughts and emotions. She'd suffered too much at his hands, she thought bitterly. She was determined that it should never happen again.

With his long stride, Patrick caught up with her as she reached the outer doors. 'Doing something exciting with your afternoon, Sister?' he asked lightly, pushing open one of the glass doors for her to exit. 'You seem to be in a hurry.'

Sarah was puzzled by his persistence. It must be obvious that she didn't like him, had no time for him and didn't want to linger in empty conversation with him.

'Only shopping . . . '

'Then you must be running away from me,' he drawled, smiling, his dark eyes glowing with the warm admiration and intent that other women had always found irresistible. It didn't melt a fraction of the frost that surrounded the slim and decidedly attractive Sister Sweet.

'Not at all,' she returned coldly, slightly scornful. 'My free time is merely much too precious to waste.'

'I agree that it should be well spent,' he said, unabashed. 'So why don't we relax over a drink in the Kingfisher? It should be fairly quiet at this hour.'

Sarah stopped short and stared. 'Why?'

Patrick laughed, far from disconcerted by the directness of her tone, the militant challenge in the sparkling sapphire eyes. 'Why not?'

She shook her head. 'I can't avoid you on the ward, Mr Egan. It's one of the drawbacks to the job. But I don't have to spend a single moment in your company at any other time, I'm glad to say.'

He raised an amused eyebrow. 'You might enjoy it, you know.'

She froze him with the ice in her eyes. 'I wouldn't enjoy it at all,' she told him firmly, with finality.

Their eyes met and held for a moment. Then Patrick shrugged broad shoulders, admitting defeat. 'Just as you like . . . ' He turned and walked away from her with his long stride, heading for the staff car park.

She had right on her side, Sarah reminded herself almost defensively, following more slowly. It would have been the height of folly to seem even the least bit encouraging, and to have gone with him for that suggested drink would have been utter madness.

The less she had to do with the surgeon, now or ever, the better it must be, she told herself. She had no reason to think of him with any warmth when she recalled how casually he'd treated her, how carelessly he'd dismissed her, and what it had done to the pride and self-respect of an inexperienced and very sensitive eighteen-year-old. She'd never forgiven him. She'd never give him another opportunity to hurt and humiliate her.

He *must* be at a loose end to have invited her to join him for a drink, she thought bitterly. It had always been much too obvious that she wasn't really his type . . .

Her car was parked a short distance from his bronze Jaguar. She produced her keys and slid into the driving seat. Much to her annoyance, nothing happened when she turned the key in the ignition. She tried again and the engine spluttered feebly and died. She waited for a moment or two, fuming.

The car was usually so reliable, and it was galling that it should play up just when she wished to get away from the man who sat behind the wheel of his smoothly purring Jaguar, obviously waiting for her to drive out of the car park.

Sarah turned the ignition key once more without result. The surgeon switched off his car engine and got out in one swift, fluid movement that belied his height and those impressive shoulders. He walked over and bent to speak to her through the open window.

'You seem to be having some trouble. Anything I can do, Sister?'

It was unexpected — and generous in view of the way she'd just slapped him down. But Sarah didn't even glance at him as she tried again to fire the reluctant engine. 'I can manage, thanks.'

It was another snub and the dark eyes narrowed. 'Aren't you being rather childish?' he drawled, not unkindly, but with an unmistakable touch of impatience in the deep voice.

'Don't let me keep you, Mr Egan. Your time is just as valuable as mine and I really don't need your assistance,' she said briskly.

'I know something about cars and their innards,' he persisted. 'I can probably get you going with very little time or trouble. All it needs is a smile from you and a '*Yes, please, Patrick*'. If that isn't too much to expect from Sister Sour — on or off duty?'

Sarah coloured slightly at the light-hearted use of the hurtful nickname. 'Just go away, will you!' she snapped.

'Sister Stubborn, too, apparently,' he added, still smiling. But he was annoyed that she had rejected another offer of the olive branch. He wished he knew what crime he'd committed in the long-ago that she found so impossible to forgive. He wished he knew what had suddenly sparked an interest in Sarah Sweet, too. He liked his women to be warm and soft, appealing and responsive to his charm and his sensuality. This girl was cold and hard and snubbing at every turn, determined to dislike him. Why the devil was he bothering to even try to thaw her out?

Glowering, Sarah got out of the car, slammed and locked the door and then brushed past him without another word, making her way back towards the hospital and a telephone. She'd call a garage and get a mechanic to come and fix her car, she decided. She didn't need Patrick Egan's help or advice — or his snide remarks!

Sister Sour, was she? That was scarcely surprising when all her lovely hopes and dreams had turned sour at a touch from him! *Sister Stubborn*, was she? He'd find out just how stubbornly she could cling to a well-founded dislike and the memory of a night when he'd given her very good cause to despise him!

It cost Sarah several pounds to learn that there was dirt in the carburettor of her car. It cost her the better part of her few hours off duty, too. So she wasn't in the best of moods when she returned to Mallory Ward at the end of visiting hours.

She swept the length of the ward,

looking for fault and having no difficulty in finding it. Having summarily banished the last of the lingering visitors and dealt with a couple of gossiping juniors, she called Helen Champion into the office.

'It seems that I can't leave my ward for an hour without coming back to utter chaos,' she said coldly, very angry, the ice in her eyes and voice reducing the staff nurse to silence. 'What has been going on here, Staff?' She didn't wait for her to attempt an answer. 'I found Mrs Lowther wandering about the day room although she's ordered complete bed rest. Can you explain that to me, please?'

'I'm very sorry, Sister . . . ' Helen found her voice with an effort. She'd never seen the ward sister look quite so stern or sound so angry. 'I'm afraid no one saw her get out of bed . . . '

'Mrs Paterson had a box of sweets on her locker yet every nurse on the ward knows that she isn't allowed sugar in any shape or form,' Sarah swept on, brushing aside both apology and attempt at explanation. 'Can you explain that to me, please?'

'I don't think her husband realises . . .'

Sarah over-rode the words. 'Miss Carter was dancing about the ward in a wisp of chiffon nightie for the delight of every man in sight and not one nurse apparently did anything but giggle at her antics. No, don't interrupt me, Nurse! I haven't finished!' The staff nurse closed the mouth that she'd unwisely ventured to open.

'There were nine people about Mrs Wilson's bed instead of the regulation two and I shall expect her blood pressure to be sky-high as a result. Perhaps you would like to explain that to Dr Freeman? You certainly owe *me* an explanation, Nurse Champion. As I came back early to find the ward turned into a bear-garden in a very short time, I'm wondering what usually goes on in my absence!'

Helen looked suitably chastened. 'I'm very sorry, Sister . . .'

'So you should be!' Sarah was unimpressed by the demure tone and manner and disappointed with the way Helen had failed to run the ward that afternoon. 'As senior nurse, it's your responsibility to see that the juniors get on with their work and that patients and their visitors behave themselves. You know that perfectly well, Staff. I hope you aren't courting popularity at the expense of ward discipline!'

'No, Sister.'

Sarah studied her thoughtfully. 'Where were you while all this was going on? In my sitting-room with your feet up?'

'No, Sister!' It was indignantly defensive. 'I was in the side ward with Mrs Nelson for some of the time. Beverley James was vomiting and distressed and I called Mr Wyman to the ward. He gave her an injection and stayed for a while. I've been occupied with other patients, too.'

'You weren't short of staff. Where was Nurse Goss?'

'I sent her off with toothache. I

told Nurse Garrard to keep an eye on things, but I'm afraid the juniors take advantage of her good nature.'

'Meaning that she can't handle them and they do exactly as they please!' Sarah said tartly.

'I'm afraid things did get rather out of hand . . . '

'But you mustn't allow things to get out of hand. I don't care how busy you are! You're acting Sister when I'm out of the ward and that means that you *supervise* and *delegate* and keep order. It doesn't mean that you run round in circles doing the work of the juniors while they gossip and giggle in the sluice and kitchen and linen cupboard! Keep *them* busy and involved and you'll find that you have plenty of time to run the ward properly.'

'Yes, Sister. I'm very sorry, Sister.'

Sarah sighed. 'Very well, Staff. Please see that it doesn't happen again. Carry on with your work while I have a look at Mrs Nelson. I shall rely on you to have the ward back to normal by the time I'm ready to do the medicine round . . . '

Sarah looked after the departing staff nurse, puzzled. Helen was usually so reliable and trustworthy. What had happened to her that afternoon? Could it be anything to do with the carelessly dropped information that Jeff Wyman had spent some time on the ward? He was good-looking and personable and he seemed to be something of a flirt. Had he been flirting with Helen, distracting her from her work and interfering with the running of the ward despite the clear warning Sarah had issued that such behaviour would be unacceptable?

She wasn't sure if she disliked the thought that he might have flouted that warning or the thought that he might be more interested in Helen than in herself . . .

4

Sarah found the pretty schoolgirl much more comfortable since the new registrar had prescribed and personally administered a drug to combat her sickness. The vomiting had briefly roused the girl from her lethargy, but now she had lapsed back into near-unconsciousness and it took Sarah some time to wake her sufficiently to get answers to her questions.

They weren't very lucid answers and Beverley's speech was slurred. Feeling that something was not quite right with the patient, Sarah made a note on the chart for the houseman to read when she did her evening round. Despite the fact that Jeff Wyman had recently seen Beverley, there was a slight niggle of anxiety about the girl at the back of Sarah's mind.

She made her way to the side ward to

check on Mrs Nelson. The old lady had undergone extensive abdominal surgery a few days earlier and was seriously ill with no hope of recovery. Having nursed many terminally ill patients during her years at Hartlake, Sarah recognised that the spark of life was fast fading and so she decided to remain with Mrs Nelson for the time being while Helen did the medicine round with a third-year nurse to check the dosage and the drug or medicine with the patient's chart before it was given.

Sarah had become fond of the elderly widow who'd been so cheerful and uncomplaining until the steady increase of pain-relieving drugs meant that she spent most of the days and nights drifting in and out of unconsciousness. Now there was little they could do for her but nurse her with tender loving care and ensure that she wasn't alone in the last hours of her life. As she had no family or friends to sit with her, it was one more nursing duty that was cheerfully undertaken by the ward staff.

Nurses weren't encouraged to become emotionally involved with patients. But patients were *people*, and Sarah's liking and concern for people had brought her into nursing. She had never found it possible to remain completely detached from all of the patients in her care throughout her years at Hartlake. Some patients sorely tried her patience and some tugged at the strings of her tender heart, but she did her best to treat them all exactly the same.

She remained with Mrs Nelson for some time, talking quietly and reassuringly to the frail little woman although she knew perfectly well that only a few of the words got through the mists that surrounded her patient. But the sound of her voice and the warm clasp of her hand were an essential comfort.

For the rest of the afternoon, Sarah was in and out of the side ward, observing Mrs Nelson's decline as well as keeping a careful eye on the juniors, noting the slightly subdued mood of the ward and ensuring its smooth running.

Mrs Nelson gave up the tenuous hold on life and slipped away without causing the least trouble to anyone. Sarah went off duty rather later than usual, glad that she hadn't failed in her promise to be with the old lady at the end. She felt rather more emotional about the loss of Mrs Nelson than she wished anyone to know. Sisters were supposed to be briskly matter-of-fact about such routine matters as birth and death, but her emotions had been much too near the surface all day for some unaccountable reason, she admitted wryly.

Having already handed over responsibility for the ward to Audrey Crane, she merely paused by the open office door to announce her departure and to exchange 'good nights' with the night staff nurse. Then she made her way through the still-bustling hospital, feeling tired and just a little depressed and dispirited.

She was distinctive in the traditional dark blue dress and fluted cap, and her glowing good looks always attracted attention. Modest Sarah assumed that it was her obvious youth for a very responsible post that drew glances and interested comment from the people she passed. She couldn't be unaware of her physical attractions, of course. But she attached very little importance to the impact of her face and figure on others.

Main Hall was crowded at that hour with the influx of friends and relatives arriving for visiting, and there was the usual milling of people about the big reception desk. Passing, Sarah caught Jimmy's eye and smiled, wondering as she always did if the big man ever went off duty and thinking how long it seemed since she'd returned his cheerful greeting that morning. It had been a long and oddly eventful day.

A tall, dark-haired and much too

attractive man lounged by the desk, surveying the scene as if he had all the time in the world to stand and stare. Seeing Sarah, he straightened, and the dark eyes glowed with the beginnings of a smile. She looked through him as if he was invisible. A frown immediately chased the smile from the depths of the deep-set and very striking eyes, and he moved forward to intercept her.

'You're late tonight, Sister,' he said in his deep, pleasant drawl.

Sarah paused and looked up into the handsome face, slightly surprised and instantly on the defensive, wondering if he'd waited in Main Hall to waylay her — and why. She wondered what he was doing at the hospital at this unusual hour, too.

'Mrs Nelson died. I stayed with her while I was needed,' she said briefly.

Patrick nodded, understanding. A good nurse never watched the clock and often worked unofficial and unpaid overtime. The care of a patient couldn't be abruptly abandoned just because she was due to go off duty, after all. Doctors found it difficult to get away on time, too. It was one of the drawbacks of the job, and one reason why doctors usually went out with nurses who knew and understood the problems and made allowances for their lateness and occasional failure to turn up for a date.

'I thought we should lose her very soon. Well, we did all we could for her. We might have been able to do so much more if she'd consulted her doctor at the first sign of trouble. Surgery should be curative rather than mere confirmation of an obvious diagnosis and prognosis.' He sighed, shrugging broad shoulders in the expensive tweed jacket. 'I hate such cases.'

The quiet passion of the words moved Sarah, for all her resolve not to warm to him. She had no reason to like him, but she had to admire a caring and concerned surgeon who continued to take an interest even when his part was played and he'd handed over the care of his patient to the nursing staff.

'She was a dear soul who didn't like to bother anyone with her aches and pains, and she had no family to insist that she saw a doctor. It isn't an unusual story, of course. I think that's one of the tragedies of our times. There are too many old people living on their own with no one to care . . . ' She broke off abruptly, threatened by a surge of emotion.

The quiver in the soft voice and the sparkle of tears in the sapphire eyes surprised Patrick. He knew she was an excellent nurse and a capable organiser, but he'd doubted the depth of her caring. Observing her in the few weeks since she'd taken over the running of Mallory Ward, she'd seemed to him to be cold and impersonal and even hard. *Sister Sour*, as the juniors declared. Now, he wondered if he'd been misled by the detachment and efficiency of the trained nurse and overlooked the warmth of the heart that beat beneath the bib of her starched apron. And maybe he'd been influenced by the chilly dislike and reserve in her manner towards himself, he admitted fairly. It was an attitude that he was increasingly determined to change if he could.

'Well . . . good night, Mr Egan.' Sarah made a move to walk on.

She was so obviously disinclined to linger in conversation with him that Patrick perversely set out to detain her. 'How's the car, Sister? Did you sort out the problem? I'll be glad to help if you're still having trouble.'

'It's fine now, thanks. The local garage said it was the carburettor . . .' Her words and tone were cool, her manner dismissive. After weeks of formal and impersonal indifference, he suddenly seemed to be taking an interest. It wasn't welcome. It was six years too late, Sarah thought bitterly.

'No doubt they charged the earth to tell you so and put it right. I could have fixed it and enjoyed doing it, you know. Cars are a hobby with me. But you're

81

fiercely independent, aren't you?' His sudden smile was warm, friendly.

Sarah consciously resisted that very dangerous charm. 'I've always found that it pays to solve my problems for myself rather than rely on the doubtful assistance of your sex, Mr Egan,' she said briskly.

He raised an amused eyebrow. 'That sounds very anti-men.'

She smiled coolly. 'Oh, I'm not anti-men. Some of them have their uses.'

'Just anti-me, perhaps?' It was soft and mocking and the dark eyes held a twinkling challenge.

Sarah looked up at him with scornful eyes. 'Heavens no! You aren't so important,' she said to crushing effect, and walked away from him, heading for the exit.

Patrick was far from crushed as he stood looking after her, that slight smile still lingering about his sensual mouth and in the depths of his dark eyes.

For weeks he'd taken little notice

of Sarah Sweet except to wonder occasionally at the obvious and apparently unfounded dislike in her attitude to himself. Suddenly, unexpectedly, he'd been jolted into new awareness and appreciation of a warm and disturbing and very appealing femininity. Now he found himself wanting her with a force that astonished him.

Light loving had always played a very necessary part in the life of a hard-working and ambitious surgeon. Total commitment to one woman was no part of his plans for the future, and he'd never met any woman who promised to be of more importance than his work or his hopes of an eventual consultancy. He didn't feel that he'd met her now in the shape of a lovely ward sister who wasn't inclined to meet him even half-way along the road to friendship.

She was very attractive to him and he admitted to a growing interest and desire for a girl who obviously remembered a past encounter that he'd completely forgotten — and held it against him for some reason. But the way he felt about Sister Sarah Sweet, with her unexpected and unsuspected enchantment, wasn't loving or anything like it, Patrick told himself confidently. He wasn't the type to indulge in foolish and futile emotion of that nature. If he ever loved at all, he'd take good care to choose someone who didn't keep him at such a chilly and determined distance, he decided carelessly, and turned at the sound of his name. Harriet Blake hurried up to him with a slightly breathless apology for keeping him waiting, amber eyes smiling at him in obvious admiration and encouragement that compensated slightly for the rebuff he'd just suffered at another woman's hands.

Holding open one of the swing doors for a young man supported by crutches and with his foot in plaster, Sarah glanced over her shoulder at just the right moment to observe that meeting between the surgeon and the new house officer. It looked like a prearranged appointment and she felt an unexpected pang of dismay.

She felt it again some minutes later as she drove out of the car park, turned into the High Street and braked to a halt at a zebra crossing, only to see that among the pedestrians who'd brought the traffic to a standstill were Patrick and Harriet Blake. The constant stream of people held her up for a few moments and she watched as the surgeon ushered the girl before him into the Kingfisher, the local pub that was a favourite with the medical staff.

Harriet Blake was so lovely and so sure of herself and so obviously Patrick Egan's type that Sarah mocked the absurd fancy that he'd been showing a degree of interest in a ward sister who kept him at a careful distance. It was just as well that he preferred women like the blonde house officer and Audrey Crane, she told herself firmly. For she certainly didn't want him to want her, to pursue her, to see her as a possible conquest all over again. The man was too attractive for any woman's peace of mind and she wasn't at all sure that she would be able to keep him at bay if he did set out to captivate her with his undeniable charm and seduce her into surrender once more.

For six years her emotions had lain dormant, untroubled by any of the men she met, on or off duty. Now, in the space of one short day, her heart had quickened at a smile from a stranger — and her wilful body had quickened all over again for a man who ought to have stayed a stranger.

She hastily thrust the thought of Patrick Egan from her with a little shudder rippling down her spine. She didn't want to remember the memories that still had the power to disturb her dreams so that she woke with her body on fire and face wet with tears. She had good reason to dislike and despise him and to distrust feelings that he'd once evoked too swiftly to his sensual and utterly selfish advantage.

So it was shattering to discover that she could still be fired by that very dangerous desire . . .

★ ★ ★

Sarah rented a small flat in a tall apartment building that was only a short drive from Hartlake but often seemed to be worlds away from that famous hospital. Liz frequently urged her to move in with her and another nurse and share expenses as well as the social life that she loved. But Sarah felt that she had enough of shop and grapevine gossip and her fellow nurses, and she liked to escape from reminders of her job, much as she loved it, at the end of a busy day on the ward.

She was fond of Liz, but her friend couldn't understand her lack of interest in men and marriage, and she was an incorrigible matchmaker. So that was one very good reason for turning down the well-meant suggestion of sharing, Sarah felt, knowing that Liz would make it her life's work to produce eligible young men for her inspection and approval at every opportunity.

Sarah wasn't lonely or unhappy in her solitude. She had friends to visit and to entertain, her books, the music she loved, the flat to run and her job at Hartlake. There was no room for romance in her busy life, even if she'd had the inclination for it. She was content with the way things were, she frequently assured the kind and concerned and warm-hearted theatre sister who was almost the only other nurse from her particular set who still remained on the staff of the famous hospital.

But that evening the flat seemed cold and empty and unwelcoming to the strangely dispirited Sarah, and she was abruptly reminded of Mrs Nelson's lonely and unloved existence in a bleak council flat. A depressing picture of herself in a similar plight at some future date leaped into her mind and she hastily banished it, telling herself sensibly that old age was many years distant and that anything could happen in the meantime.

She might even get married. There was really no reason why she shouldn't put the past behind her for good and look for a man she could love, one who would love her in return and wish to marry her, after all. One mistake didn't have to blight her life for ever. Anyone could make a mistake. It was making the same mistake twice that was totally unforgivable, and Sarah had no intention of doing that!

Perhaps it had been more than foolish to hold every admiring and interested man at more than arm's length all these years. But she'd been so afraid of repeating the mistake she'd made when she allowed Patrick Egan's arms to close about her and the magic of his kisses to sweep her completely off her feet.

All of a sudden she felt as if she

was ready to step out of the shadows
of that past and disastrous involvement
and look upon a man as a possible
friend and companion and even lover,
rather than a threat. It might be absurd,
but she felt that she had Jeff Wyman to
thank for that and she wondered what it
was about the red-headed registrar that
had so unexpectedly broken through all
her instinctive defences.

Whatever it was, she knew that she
liked him and she was prepared to trust
him more than any man she'd known
in a very long time. Her spirits lifted at
the thought of the party he was giving
and the invitation he'd issued. It was
some time since she'd been to a party
of any kind, and perhaps she needed
to feel that there might be more to
life than hard work and dedication to
nursing, with only the promise of a
lonely old age at the end of it all.

Like many women, Sarah wanted to
love and be loved and to know the
fulfilment of marriage and motherhood
one day. Like many nurses, she felt

that a doctor would be a very suitable husband. So maybe Jeff Wyman had come into her life at just the right moment . . .

* * *

Arriving on Mallory the next morning at her usual early time, Sarah was surprised to learn that the new registrar was already on the ward. She glanced swiftly along the row of beds to the drawn curtains that concealed surgeon and patient from curious eyes.

'Crisis?' she asked quickly, turning to the staff nurse. Her arrival had interrupted Audrey Crane in the task of writing up the report in readiness for handing over to the day staff.

Audrey nodded. 'Beverley James. We couldn't rouse her at all this morning.'

'So you called Mr Wyman. That was sensible,' Sarah approved almost absently, her thoughts racing.

'He left instructions last night that we were to call him right away if she didn't react to the usual stimuli.'

'Oh, I see. Very well, Staff. I'll go and talk to him while you complete the report . . . '

An unsmiling Jeff Wyman glanced round as she slipped between the brightly-coloured curtains. 'I'm transferring Beverley to the IC Unit for neurosurgical observation,' he announced directly. 'She's a very sick girl.'

Sarah's heart sank at the confirmation of an anxiety that had been at the back of her mind since the girl came back from Theatres. 'Coma?'

'Looks like it.'

She sighed. 'I had my suspicions. She never came round fully at any time, you know. I made a note on the chart.'

'Yes, I know you did. I read it.' Jeff pulled thoughtfully at his lower lip with long fingers, watching as Sarah bent over the unconscious girl, seeking for the pulse that beat so slowly and almost imperceptibly in the slender wrist, lifting the heavy lids to check the pupils. 'With any luck it's infective, and we can start to do something about it as soon as the bacillus has been isolated and identified by the lab experts,' he went on briskly. 'I'd rather think that than suspect a slip-up by myself or the anaesthetist during surgery, but we have to consider all the possibilities, of course. Needless to say, a full investigation by the powers-that-be is already under way — and it didn't need an irate father to get things moving,' he added with a slight grimace.

'Mr James? Is he here?'

'In your sitting-room, I believe. I felt we should advise the parents that there is some cause for concern in Beverley's condition and he was at the hospital within twenty minutes, out for someone's blood. Mine, preferably, I gather.'

Sarah sympathised with his feelings. First day in a new job and first operation for a new surgical registrar — and something had apparently gone very wrong. It was a natural reaction for the surgeon to wonder if he had been at fault — and it was equally natural that the family should wonder the same thing.

'I don't believe that you are responsible,' she said quickly, stoutly. 'You had Patrick Egan breathing down your neck all the time you were operating, didn't you? He'd have known it immediately if you were putting the patient at risk in any way whatever, and he'd have taken over from you without a moment's hesitation. I'm sure he'll be able to set your mind at rest if you talk to him.'

'Yes, I expect you're right. I'll do that. Thanks, Sister.' A glimmer of his warm smile dawned in the grey eyes. 'You've made me feel very much better. Oh, I can't blame the father for being upset and alarmed, of course. His daughter comes in for a routine appendicectomy that turns out to be something more complicated and then lapses into coma for no obvious cause.

He wants answers to his questions and we aren't in a position to supply them at present.'

'But you will be soon,' she assured him.

'Well, I hope to have one or two results of yesterday's tests within an hour or so.'

Sarah remembered the various investigations he'd ordered that were not usual practice following surgery.

'You felt that something was wrong, too, didn't you? You kept a very close watch on her yesterday afternoon.'

'I had a hunch. I should have acted on it right away instead of waiting and hoping I was wrong,' he said wryly. 'Are you any good at handling difficult relatives, Sister? Will you keep Mr James off my back for an hour at least while I rustle up some answers?'

'I'll do my best. I expect I've had more practice than you,' she told him lightly, smiling at him.

'You're a nice girl, Sarah,' he said softly, too low for anyone else's ears.

'I like you a lot . . .'

His lips briefly brushed her cheek, startling her, and then he whisked through the curtains and hurried along the ward to the office to make a call to the Intensive Care Unit and hurry along the transfer of his patient from Mallory. Sarah put her hand to her glowing cheek, a slight smile trembling on her lips. He was a very nice man, she decided. She liked *him* a lot, too.

She'd been in two minds about going to his party that evening. Now she was determined to be there if it was still on. He might not be in any mood for entertaining old and new friends at the end of a day that would obviously be filled with anxiety for a young surgeon who hoped to make his mark at the world-famous Hartlake Hospital . . .

5

Beverley James was transferred to the IC Unit without delay and Sarah soothed the anxious Mr James and did her best to reassure him and convince him that the doctors would soon know what was wrong with his daughter and treat her accordingly.

Meanwhile, the night nurses were thankfully handing over the business of endless and repetitious ward rounds to the day staff and going off to their beds. Sarah returned to the office in time for Report and to take the reins from Audrey Crane.

The morning proved to be quieter and more uneventful than its beginning had suggested. Sarah managed to catch up with some of her paperwork while her nurses got on with their routine tasks. There were no new admissions that day and no one listed for surgery, and three patients were discharged.

It wasn't one of Patrick Egan's operating days and so he had no need to visit the ward. Harriet Blake did the round in record time that morning and Sarah wasn't impressed by the woman's attitude to her work. Maybe she was destined to be brilliant in the operating theatre, but she seemed to lack the humanity and the genuine interest and compassion that were so necessary to the make-up of a good nurse or a conscientious doctor. Surgeons who didn't care were merely clever technicians, Sarah always felt — and, like every big hospital with a number of surgical firms on its staff, Hartlake had its quota of those.

For all his other faults, Patrick Egan *cared*. Sarah had observed that during the weeks of working with him on Mallory, and the knowledge had slightly undermined her resolve to regard him with loathing and contempt until the end of time. She could never, never like him again or want anything to do with him off the ward, of course. But she couldn't help a sneaking admiration and respect for the surgeon, even if she had no time at all for the man.

Towards the end of the morning Jeff Wyman came back to the ward, and Sarah looked up with a quick warm smile for him as he entered the office. She laid down her pen. 'Any news?'

'Yes — and it's good,' he said blithely. 'We've got a result that's told us what we needed to know. It's a rare condition. Multiple neurogenic shock. Reaction to the anaesthetic caused her nervous system to virtually close down. It's something that no one could have foreseen and it isn't anyone's fault, thank God! Now we know what's wrong she's already getting the proper treatment and the prognosis is optimistic. But she's going to need special nursing for some days.'

'Could she have died?'

He perched on the corner of her desk with a very sober expression in his grey eyes. 'Certainly . . . if we hadn't

99

managed to track down the cause of her collapse as quickly as we did. Her respiratory system was already ceasing to function properly and we had to put her into an oxygen tent. Hopefully there shouldn't be any lasting pleural or neural damage and Matthews doesn't think there's any actual brain damage involved. You were right about Egan, by the way. He was very kind to the new boy, very supportive.'

Sarah smiled at him. 'You must be relieved.'

Jeff grinned. 'You can call that the understatement of the year! I didn't know whether I ought to resign right away or wait to be struck off!'

He made light of the matter in probably characteristic manner, but Sarah could imagine just how anxious the young surgeon must have been and what it meant to him to be cleared of any suspicion of negligence. 'Even more cause for celebration tonight, now,' she suggested.

He looked at her blankly for a

moment. Then he leaped to his feet, clapping a hand to his brow in almost comically classic fashion. 'Good God! The party! I'd forgotten all about it. The advent of the five thousand!'

Sarah laughed. 'You've a lot of friends!' she teased lightly.

'Yes . . . and they'll be bringing *their* friends, I dare say. I must dash away and buy a few gallons of beer and several tons of fish-paste. It ought to be champagne and caviar but I can't afford that on a junior registrar's pay!' He paused in the doorway. 'You will be coming, I hope, Sister?' The formal address was accompanied by such a twinkle of merriment that she knew it was only for the benefit of a passing junior. The smile in the grey eyes and the softening of his voice turned the official term into a near-endearment.

The surgeon didn't wait for an answer. Perhaps he felt it was likely to be *no* and he didn't want to hear it . . .

Sarah was torn between a wish to

go to the party, mingle with people and get to know the very likeable Jeff Wyman outside the clinical confines of the ward, and a reluctance to seem too interested in and encouraging of a man she'd only just met. He seemed to like her and seemed to want to draw her into some kind of relationship. But he seemed to like everyone with that easy, good-natured affability and charm, and he was making quite an impact on several of her nurses, she knew. Helen Champion, for one.

Sarah had no intention of competing for any man's interest with her junior nurses . . .

However, she did go to the party. It was some minutes before she could find a place to park among the cars that lined the narrow street of tall houses that had been mostly converted into flats. The hospital was conveniently close and the rents were said to be reasonable, and so the flats in Clifton Street were much sought after by the medical and nursing staff of Hartlake.

The top-floor flat that Jeff had taken over from his predecessor on Sir Lionel's surgical firm was bustling with people and loud with music, and Sarah almost turned tail as she hesitated on the threshold. But Jeff caught sight of her and came to greet her with such a warm smile that her heart and spirits promptly rose.

'You came,' he said simply, as though her arrival had completed the evening's enjoyment for him.

Sarah was suddenly glad that she'd made the considerable effort to overcome her reluctance. 'You invited me,' she reminded him.

'But I didn't expect you,' he told her frankly. He put a casual arm about her shoulders. 'I'm really glad to see you, Sarah. Where's the boyfriend?'

She shook her head. 'I'm on my own.' There was no need to explain that she didn't have a boyfriend. She felt sure that he'd already learned through the hospital grapevine that

Sister Sour had no time for men — and she hoped she wasn't simply a challenge to a young surgeon who prided himself on his acquisition of conquests. Somehow he didn't strike her as that type, but one never really knew, she told herself sensibly.

'Even better,' he approved. 'Let's get you a drink and introduce you to some people.' He drew her across the room towards a makeshift bar. 'It's going to be a mad night, but I'll look after you . . .'

Sarah hoped that he meant that promise, but within minutes he'd left her side as more guests arrived. She stood in the midst of a crowd of unknowns, sipping a rather dubious punch, conscious of curious glances. Everyone else at the party seemed to be a friend or colleague from the hospital in North London that Jeff had left to come to work at Hartlake, and she felt that a Hartlake nurse — and a ward sister to boot! — stuck out like a sore thumb. Sisters were never popular guests at such affairs, in any case, she thought dryly.

He'd introduced her to people like a dutiful host, but they'd drifted away and Sarah wondered if she had two heads or simply too little to say for herself. She was out of practice when it came to parties, she admitted. No doubt she seemed stiff and cold and unfriendly when she was only slightly shy. But no one ever expected a state registered nurse to be shy and unsure of herself, she knew. And no one ever believed that a ward sister was human!

Some moments later, she saw two of her nurses from Mallory among a cluster of new arrivals. Helen Champion was looking cool and fresh and pretty in peppermint green silk and she was welcomed like a long-lost love by an effusive Jeff. Watching and listening, Sarah felt a foolish pang. But, liking him, she didn't want to discover that he was just another smooth-tongued charmer whom she ought not to trust.

Audrey Crane looked sexy and sensational in short-skirted, low-cut pink chiffon that left little to the imagination and had almost every man in the room edging nearer in the hope of an introduction. She was clinging to Patrick Egan's arm and he was smiling down at her with obvious enjoyment of her impact on others and amusement at the envy of other men.

Sarah looked at the couple coldly, unimpressed by the striking good looks and charisma of the tall man in cream slacks and shirt and casual leather jacket, scorning to feel even the slightest flicker of jealousy of the blonde staff nurse but marvelling that *she'd* ever managed to attract even the fleeting interest of someone like Patrick Egan. She had been shy and unsure of herself in *those* days, too. A quiet and modest girl with little experience of men, who'd been swept off her feet by the flattery of his smiling attentions and the expertise of his love-making. She'd been a very green girl, too, she thought with a sudden welling of bitterness, remembering that she'd stupidly supposed that a brief encounter might be the beginning of a lifetime of mutual loving. But he hadn't even recognised her at their next meeting . . .

Jeff came back to her with another glass of punch and an apology for neglecting her and a promise to give her all his attention as soon as he could — and then was gone again as someone called him from across the room. A few moments later, Sarah saw him with an arm about Helen's waist and she wondered if he was saying much the same things to her staff nurse with the same degree of doubtful sincerity. It seemed that he smiled and spoke with flattering warmth of eager friendliness to every girl he met, and her heart sank slightly.

'*Hello!* What are *you* doing here!' Audrey Crane's astonishment was unconsciously offensive. Somehow, people were finding room to dance, trampling ruthlessly on anyone in their way, and she was in a strange man's arms in front of Sarah as the music stopped abruptly. 'This is fun, isn't it?' she swept on effusively. 'The best party I've been to in ages!'

Sarah smiled coolly, non-committal. The staff nurse had either lost or shaken off her boyfriend, but she was getting plenty of attention from other men, she thought dryly. She turned to put her glass on a high shelf, safe from a careless elbow. There had already been a few breakages, each one greeted by loud cries of delight from the rather unruly crowd.

Sarah wasn't a kill-joy but it wasn't her kind of party and they weren't her kind of people. She wondered if it was too soon to make an excuse to Jeff and leave. She'd had enough of the noise, the confusion and the painful sense of isolation, and she felt that she couldn't rely on Jeff's promises after all.

Turning to look for him, she collided with a tall man whose shoulder roughly brushed against her cheek as he hastily moved out of the way of someone with an unsteady trayful of overflowing glasses.

'Sorry . . . !' Patrick had a warm smile and a swift murmur of apology and a steadying hand on her bare arm before he realised that it was Sarah. 'I didn't know that you were here, Sister . . . ' he said slowly and with too-obvious surprise. He'd scarcely recognised the slender girl in the multi-coloured silk frock, dark hair loose and clinging on her shoulders and framing the delicate oval of a rather lovely face.

Sarah shook off his strong hand, stung by the formal address although she'd have instantly resented the familiar use of her first name. 'I'm just leaving,' she said coolly, looking at him with a militant gleam in her eyes, venting on him the absurd disappointment in an evening that had seemed to hold so much promise when she put on the new frock, took pains with her face and hair and drove through the damp and darkening streets to this party.

'I didn't expect to see you here,' he repeated, wondering how he'd missed her even in the crowd. She was distinctive, very attractive, with an air that seemed to set her apart from every other girl in the room. Perhaps it was that hint of reserve and reticence and the touch-me-not coolness of attitude that drew him like a magnet, he thought, intrigued. Whatever it was, his senses were stirring and he wanted her warm and willing in his arms.

'Well, you *haven't* seen me, have you?' It was tart.

Patrick smiled down at her. 'It's hard to find anyone in this kind of crush.'

'Particularly when you've no reason to look.' Sarah didn't know why she bothered to bandy words with him and allow him to delay her from leaving. The evening might have been so much better spent, she thought crossly, annoyed with herself for foolish expectations.

Looking into the sparkling sapphire eyes, Patrick suddenly experienced the oddest sensation of *déjà vu*. Somewhere, sometime, this had happened before, he felt. Somewhere, sometime, they'd met like this at a party and he'd known the sudden, compelling force of attraction and desire that was firing his blood all over again. He wondered why he couldn't recall the occasion or its outcome with any clarity. He ransacked his memory for pointers, without success.

It had to be all of six years since, of course — and that was a long time. In those days, Sarah Sweet had been a first-year nurse and he'd been an ambitious young surgeon, making the most of his opportunities with nurses he met in the course of his work as a necessary release and relaxation after the demands of long days on the ward or in Theatres.

Somewhere, sometime, their paths

had crossed and he'd committed the crime that he couldn't recall and she wasn't prepared to forgive and forget. Now she was snubbing him as usual, but he felt compelled to make one more attempt to break through the barrier of her hostility. He was naturally curious to know how he'd offended in the past, but it suddenly seemed much more important that they should be friends in the future. And maybe more . . .

'Well, now that I have found you, let me get you a drink,' he suggested lightly. 'Or is someone already looking after you . . . ?'

Sarah ignored the tentative probing of his tone. 'I don't want a drink, thanks. I'm on the point of leaving.' She looked round for the elusive Jeff, anxious to escape.

'So soon? Don't you like parties?'

'I don't like this one,' she said bluntly.

Patrick smiled. 'Sister Stuffy,' he teased with not unkind mockery. 'Tell me what you don't like about it.'

Sarah looked at him coldly, resenting the light but meaningful rebuke of the words. 'The people.' It was pointed, deliberate.

Amusement crinkled the corners of the dark eyes. 'Some of them *are* rather young and wild,' he sympathised. 'I expect you're feeling your age, Sister. Or is it just the weight of your 'strings'? You should leave them at home when you come to a party, you know. Relax and enjoy yourself. Let your hair down,' he suggested, smiling. 'Figuratively speaking, I mean, of course. You've already done just that, in fact — and very nice it looks, too.'

With a deepening of his smile, he reached to twine his hand in the shining mass of dark hair that framed her face and turned an attractive girl into a beautiful woman. 'You don't look in the least like Sister Sour tonight, so why play the part?' he added softly.

Sarah wondered why he supposed that the anger and contempt and resentment of six years could be swept away all in a moment by the warm enchantment of that smile. She jerked from his disturbing touch and the threat of his nearness, irritated by the arrogance of a too-attractive man who thought he had only to smile to have her melt into his arms. It had happened once and she was determined that it should never happen again.

'I wish you'd expend all that famous charm on someone else,' she said cuttingly. 'It ceased to be effective a long time ago as far as I'm concerned.'

He regarded her wryly. 'You really know how to hang on to a grudge, don't you?'

She was about to turn away impatiently when suddenly Jeff was at her side, sliding an arm about her and smiling at her with warm approval and admiration and unmistakably laying claim to her for the surgeon's benefit. 'How's my lovely girl? Everything all right? The boss taking good care of you, is he?' He grinned and slapped Patrick on the back with easy familiarity. 'Look after her well for me, Pat. She's precious!' His lips skated across Sarah's cheek. 'I *will* get back to you soon, love — and then I'm all yours for the rest of the evening. That's a promise!'

He was gone again on the light words and a too-loud wave of music from the stereo drowned Sarah's instinctive protest. She looked after him doubtfully, torn between a natural dislike at being taken for granted, a foolish glow of pleasure at the meaningful warmth of liking and interest in his manner, and annoyance that it must seem to Patrick Egan that she'd lied about her relationship with the new registrar.

Jostled by a couple of too-energetic dancers, she was thrust against Patrick who promptly put a protective arm about her. Sarah stiffened and tried to pull away and felt his arm tighten against the tug of her resistance.

She glowered. 'Do you mind . . . ?'

He didn't let her go. 'Wyman seems

to have appointed me as his deputy,' he said lightly. 'I'm just taking care of you in my own inimitable way.' His smile coaxed her to soften and melt. It had seldom met with such little success, he thought, looking down at the proud and stubborn and enchantingly lovely face that threatened to tug at his heart as much as it challenged his sensuality.

'I can take care of myself.' Sarah stood stiff and reluctant, desperately fighting the swift and unwelcome tingling of the blood in her veins.

She had no intention of struggling with his obviously superior strength, but she was much too conscious of his masculinity for comfort and furious with him for taking advantage of the situation. He knew that she wasn't likely to make a scene that would draw attention to an incident that no one had yet noticed, she thought bitterly, thankful that few of their fellow guests knew that they were senior surgeon and ward sister from the nearby Hartlake

Hospital. The last thing she wanted was to have their names linked by grapevine gossip. She saw with relief that Audrey Crane was too preoccupied in encouraging her present companion to notice the activities of the surgeon who was rumoured to be her current boyfriend.

Patrick looked down at her thoughtfully. 'Wyman seems to be very popular. All these people and every one of them a bosom friend, apparently. Including you.'

Sarah's chin went up at the hint of censure in his tone. 'I hardly know him,' she said defensively.

'Then he's travelled a long way in a short time,' he said dryly, spurred by a jealous dislike of the man's success where he continually failed. 'The right kind of encouragement makes all the difference, of course.' He put his other arm about her, imprisoned her, ignoring her swift and indignant protest and the spark in the lovely sapphire eyes. 'But I'm the one who's holding you right now. Shall we shuffle with the rest of the crowd so that I have a legitimate excuse for keeping you in my arms?' A smile danced in the dark eyes.

The liquid warmth of that mischievous smile and the stirring of her senses as he held her captive in his strong embrace was a very real threat to Sarah's resolve. He was attractive, exciting, persuasive — and much too dangerous. 'Just let me go, please, Mr Egan,' she said stiffly, ice tinkling. 'I don't wish to dance.'

'My dancing deserves a much better floor and a lot more room,' he agreed smoothly, as though that was her only objection. 'I dance very well, Sister. Come with me to Founders Ball and I'll prove it to you!'

Sarah knew it wasn't a serious invitation. For a senior surgeon to take a ward sister to the Ball that was the highlight of the hospital year would be tantamount to a public declaration of interest and honourable intent. She doubted if Patrick Egan had an honourable bone in his body where women were concerned.

'I expect Nurse Crane will be very pleased to go with you,' she said indifferently.

'To hell with Nurse Crane,' he retorted.

Sarah glanced up at him, surprise flickering, wondering how the girl had offended and almost sorry for her. She knew how ruthless this man could be when it came to discarding a woman he no longer wanted. 'That's just what I'd expect from a man like you!' she said impulsively.

Patrick frowned and released her abruptly, suddenly annoyed by the seemingly senseless and persistent hostility of her attitude. 'It's a lot of hate for someone who offended such a long time ago, isn't it? Water under the bridge, Sarah! Whatever I did, I'm sorry. Surely we can put it behind us and be friends!' Dark eyes glittered with angry frustration.

Sarah was unmoved by the almost

impatient demand. Once bitten, forever shy, she told herself firmly. 'You're the last person that I'd want for a friend,' she said crisply, brushing past him. Friends were loyal, reliable and trustworthy, generous with their affection and concern. He was none of those things. Men like Patrick Egan with their dangerous sensuality and opportunist attitudes were a woman's natural enemy!

She didn't bother to look for Jeff and make her excuses as she forced her way through the crush of people to the door. She was cross with herself for warming to a man who probably bestowed his easy, smiling charm on every woman, and even more annoyed that the practised persuasions of another man had almost tempted her to relent and admit that it was foolish to harbour a grudge until the end of time.

Damn Patrick Egan!

He'd ruined her evening with his renewed impact on her senses and his lingering threat to a heart that had once been too eager to plunge into loving and paid the price.

Despising him, distrusting him, Sarah knew that she was still drawn to the too-attractive surgeon despite the lessons of the past . . .

6

'*Sarah . . . !*'

Her name, clad in the warm velvet of his deep voice and with urgency in its uttering, sounded like mingled endearment and appeal.

She'd reached the last flight of the narrow stairway and she froze with a hand on the wooden rail, heart leaping and legs turning abruptly to jelly. For absolutely no good reason, the soft sound of his voice speaking her name turned back the clock, sweeping away the years as if they'd never been.

Suddenly she was eighteen again, foolishly impressed by a man's looks and charm and physical magnetism, confused by the emotions he stirred and too inexperienced to know how to handle them to protect herself from folly — youthfully flattered by an unexpected and ardent interest and filled with romantic notions of love and happy-ever-after at a kiss.

For a moment Sarah stood as if turned to stone. Then, as Patrick came down the stairs to join her on the small landing, she swung to face him, defensive but without defence, heart hammering.

Without another word, he reached for her and his mouth came down on her own with an ardent hunger. She was shaken by the hint of anger in the way he kissed her, taking her lips as if they belonged to him, crushing her in strong arms.

His kiss was deep and demanding, swirling her senses, weakening her resolve. But her lips were cold and unresponsive and her body remained taut and unwilling in his arms. It took all her strength of mind and will to remain apparently unmoved by the power and the passion of his embrace. But she managed it . . . just!

Holding her, tasting the sweetness of her lips and thrilling to the exciting femininity of her slight body, memory stirred as desire surged on a flood of wanting.

Somewhere, sometime, he'd held her and known the willing response of her lips, the clinging warmth of her embrace, the yielding softness of her lovely body for his delight. He knew it in his bones, in the quickening of his blood, in the very depths of his being and in the uncertain mists of memory. He knew, too, that he'd felt the lack of her in his life ever since, deep down, totally unrealised until this moment.

Patrick had never been in love. Now, he wondered if he'd waited all his life to love and need the girl he was holding in his arms. There was something about her that seemed to invade his heart and melt his bones and make a nonsense of everything he'd ever thought and felt about the demands and responsibilities and commitment of loving one woman until the end of time.

He felt a deep sense of dissatisfaction

and disappointment, a fury of frustration, at his apparent failure to break down the barrier of hostility with the appeal to her senses that had never failed to succeed with other women. It seemed impossible to chip away even one small brick of the wall of resistance and resentment that stood between them.

If it had been any other woman, Patrick might have shrugged, admitted defeat and walked away. But the desire for the stubborn and spirited Sister Sweet seemed to be too insistent, too persistent, and much too powerful to be dismissed.

Lifting his dark head, he looked into the rebellious sapphire eyes. 'That isn't the first time I've kissed you,' he said softly.

Sarah thrust him away. 'It will certainly be the last!'

He raised an amused eyebrow at the tilt of her chin, the militant sparkle of her lovely eyes. 'Going to slap my face again?'

'You *do* have a bad memory, Mr

Egan!' Ignoring the gentle teasing of the words, infuriated that he had so little recollection and no understanding at all of an incident that had affected her so deeply, Sarah threw the words at him, bitterness welling to whip up the hate that had almost died on her as she stood in his arms.

His eyes narrowed at the snap of the words. 'Got it wrong, have I?' he drawled, searching for clues in the lovely and very stormy face. 'So you *didn't* slap my face all those years ago. I know I ought to remember, but I don't, I'm afraid. I wish you'd refresh my memory with a few details. Like how and when and where we met before — and why you went out of my life. I'm sure that I must have wanted you then just as much as I do now . . . ' His voice softened and warmed on the words.

Sarah looked at him coldly, reminding herself that she wasn't eighteen and impressionable any more. She was a mature and level-headed hospital sister who surely knew better than to trust the smiling eyes and smooth tongue of a dangerous charmer all over again. But her heart was hammering high in her throat and the beginning of excitement was stealing through the secret places of her slender body.

'I don't attach any importance to your kind of wanting,' she said carefully. 'Then or now. And there isn't any point in raking over details of something that was never important.' It was proud, almost defiant.

Patrick considered her thoughtfully, unconvinced. 'As I've forgotten, perhaps it was as unimportant as you claim. But you seem to have remembered.'

'Perhaps because *I* was sober at the time!' The hint of mockery in his eyes and voice goaded her into the impulsive and probably unwise retort.

The surgeon was surprised into a chuckled of laughter. 'Oh, now I'm beginning to understand,' he said, shaking his head at her in amused reproach as the pieces of the puzzle seemed to fall into place. 'Is that how it was? You *were* an innocent and an idiot if you took notice of something said or done after a few drinks! As for holding it against me all these years . . . Really, Sarah! What did I do or say that was so dreadful and so unforgettable, for heaven's sake?'

'It's water under the bridge,' she reminded him.

'So it doesn't matter, does it?'

Amusement died abruptly. 'But it *does* matter,' he said quietly. 'Whatever I did, you seem to have hated me for it ever since. There's a wall of hate between us, Sarah.'

'You care about that, of course!' Unmoved by the coaxing sound of her name and the look in his eyes, impatient and sceptical, she turned towards the stairs.

Instantly, Patrick blocked her way with his tall, powerful frame. 'Yes, I *do* care. More than you're prepared to believe. And I want it down. I want you . . . ' As he spoke, he put both hands on her shoulders and smiled into her eyes with persuasive warmth.

His touch burned through the thin silk of her frock and sent a flame of desire shafting through Sarah's body. Her hands clenched so tightly that the nails dug painful crescents into the palms. He sounded sincere but she wouldn't be swayed all over again by the ardent glow in those dark eyes.

She broke free just as Jeff came hurrying down the stairs, two at a time. 'You aren't leaving, I hope, Sarah!' It sounded like genuine dismay. 'I hope you aren't running off with my girl, Pat! I thought I could trust you to look after my interests without furthering your own! That's friendship for you!'

It was light, good-humoured banter, but there was the hint of an edge to the words that implied a dislike of having found them in obvious tête-à-tête and apparently on the point of leaving together. He slid an arm about Sarah with the air of claiming her back from a would-be rival. 'I've been trying to get to you all evening and at last I'm free to give you my undivided attention, love. You can't walk out on a great party!'

Grateful for his timely interruption and glad of a camouflage for the feelings and the fury that another man had evoked, Sarah smiled on the registrar and allowed him to sweep her back up the narrow stairway with a warmly possessive arm about her waist.

Patrick didn't follow, then or later. Sarah wondered how Audrey Crane felt about being abandoned by her boyfriend in such cavalier fashion. But as the staff nurse seemed to have found other fish to fry, perhaps an affair that had been the talk of the grapevine for some weeks was over.

Maybe the couple had quarrelled that evening.

Maybe that explained why Patrick Egan had made such a pointed play for her, meaning to use her to his own ends all over again, Sarah thought angrily.

This time, he'd failed.

This time, she'd kept her head . . .

* * *

The next morning, feeling fresher than she'd expected after a late night, Sarah rose from her desk and went to stand by the window, surveying the ward with a familiar glow of satisfaction and approval. First rounds finished, there was a brief lull in the busy morning and the first-years were taking their coffee break. The rest of her nurses were busy with dressings and sterilising instruments or attending to the needs of the seriously ill.

Sunshine slanted through the long windows to fall across newly-made beds and comfortably settled patients, tidy lockers and bed-tables and vases of bright flowers and gleaming trolleys. The ward was ready for the first of the doctors' rounds.

Even as her thoughts turned reluctantly to Patrick Egan, the ward doors swung back to admit the surgeon and his entourage.

He paused to look about him, tall and impressive and darkly handsome. The Hartlake Heart-Throb. The old, almost forgotten nickname of earlier days sprang to Sarah's mind. Apt, she thought bitterly. He'd certainly set her heart throbbing . . . with hurt, with humiliation, with anxiety and apprehension. Now it quickened with an involuntary excitement.

Sarah suppressed it angrily and went to greet the surgeon. As she approached the group, Harriet Blake said something and Patrick turned to her with his swift, too-attractive smile. The girl was determined to be noticed, Sarah thought dryly, filling with dislike.

'Good morning, Mr Egan . . . gentlemen.' Her smile swept the group of students and managed to exclude the surgeon and his new house officer.

'Good morning, Sister.'

Meeting the dark eyes, a tide of colour came and went in Sarah's face as she recalled the way he'd held and kissed her and the emotions he'd aroused all over again. There was nothing in his eyes or voice to imply that he might be remembering, too, she realised.

'We've come to make a nuisance of ourselves, I'm afraid, Sister,' he said jocularly for the benefit of his youthful students, and a ripple of amusement greeted the light words.

Sarah's smile was equally dutiful and it didn't reach the sapphire eyes. 'Not at all, Mr Egan. My patients are always pleased to see you.'

Patrick wondered why she felt it necessary to point the words with that slight emphasis. He'd always known that he wasn't a welcome visitor to the ward since she'd taken charge of it. She'd made it very obvious that she disliked and resented him. Had he really expected to overcome the chill hostility of her attitude all in a moment?

He'd spent a restless night thinking

of her, longing for her, telling himself that in the light of a new day it would seem the height of absurdity to believe that the stubborn and spirited and fiercely independent Sister Sweet was really the woman he wanted, now and for ever. Why, he scarcely knew the girl or anything about her! He wasn't even sure that he liked her — and surely he had too much pride to want a woman who seemed to have neither liking nor desire for him!

Love had come out of the blue. But it had come to stay, turning his world upside down. Now all he had to do was to persuade Sarah to love him in return. A busy hospital ward was neither the time nor the place, of course. So he was carefully impersonal, protecting her as well as himself from the all-seeing eyes and all-hearing ears of junior nurses who seemed to lurk in every corner in the hope of stumbling across such a delicious item of gossip as a romance between a surgeon and a ward sister.

'We must try not to take up too much of your valuable time, Sister,' he said, very formally and with only the ghost of a smile.

He was too formal, too impersonal. By contrast, Jeff's quick wink and mischievous gleam of a smile seemed almost outrageous as he hurried into the ward some minutes later to join the group about a patient's bed.

Sarah usually enjoyed the surgeon's teaching round and prided herself on having the history and treatment and progress of each patient clearly in mind before it began. That morning, she was much too conscious of their exchange on the previous night and she wished that she'd delegated the task of accompanying him and his team to her senior staff nurse.

Listening as Harriet Blake detailed her findings from an earlier round, Sarah admired the competent manner of the elegant blonde house officer, but she couldn't warm to her as a person. She seemed too cold and too clinical — more concerned with impressing Patrick with her cleverness than caring for the reaction of the women as she spoke about them with a detachment that relegated them to mere case histories.

At the finish of the round, the students filtered from the ward. Harriet Blake went off to fill in forms and make arrangements for various tests that Patrick wanted for certain cases and Jeff lingered at the bedside of the last patient to satisfy himself on a particular point. Sarah walked with the surgeon to the swing doors of the ward as etiquette demanded, listening carefully while he spoke of a new drug that he wanted to try on one of his patients, ready to challenge him on the possibility of side-effects. She was never afraid to oppose him or any other surgeon if she felt that a certain operation or a certain treatment was not in the best interests of a patient.

Patrick looked down at her with a

smile in the dark eyes, sensing her reservations. Her trim figure in the dark blue dress delighted his eye and his heart turned over in his breast as he saw the familiar tilt of challenge to her chin and the slight sparkle in her sapphire eyes. She was lovely and spirited and enchanting and an ache of longing stabbed at his heart and his senses.

'Mrs Spender is very old,' Sarah reminded him, commencing battle. 'Do you think it fair to experiment with something that might make her so uncomfortable that it does more harm than good, mentally if not physically? I don't like the sound of those side-effects, Mr Egan.'

'She won't consent to surgery so we must try some other method of relieving her condition. Or do you think we should simply send her home and tell her to live with it just because she's eighty-three?'

'She's already lived with it for some time, hasn't she? I don't blame her for shying from the thought of surgery. So would I!'

'Thank you for that vote of confidence, Sister,' he said, the twinkle in his eyes inviting her to share his sardonic amusement.

'Nothing personal,' she retorted, refusing to smile. 'If it was necessary, I'd put my life in your hands without the slightest hesitation.'

'I'm delighted to hear you say so.' His smile was quick and warm, almost caressing. 'We'll have dinner tonight and talk about it, shall we?'

'Surgically speaking!' She rebuffed and rebuked him with the chill of the words. 'I've every admiration for your work. Nothing more than that. We were discussing Mrs Spender,' she reminded him briskly, every inch the busy ward sister who had no time for flirtatious nonsense.

'Not the time or the place to discuss you and me, is it?' he agreed. 'But I'll get it right one day.' He spoke with a confidence that he couldn't feel, for her indifference didn't encourage him to believe that he'd ever get it right where she was concerned.

A first-year nurse came up and waited, hands locked behind her back. Sarah turned with the swift, sweet smile that she never bestowed on the surgeon. 'What is it, Nurse?'

'Would you take a call, please, Sister? It's Mr Bennett and he insists on speaking to you if possible.'

'Very well. Ask him to hold on for a few moments. Thank you, Nurse.'

'We are always being interrupted,' Patrick drawled as the junior hurried back to the ward office. 'I suspect that you arrange it that way. Send out distress signals as soon as I venture to say something that verges on the personal, do you?'

'Mrs Spender,' Sarah said very firmly.

He nodded, accepting defeat for the moment. 'Mrs Spender. As you are so concerned, I'll give it a few more days. Continue the present treatment and maybe some other solution will offer itself.'

'Then if there's nothing else . . . ?' Sarah made a slight but obvious move to leave the surgeon.

'Thank you for your time, Sister.' It was sardonic. With a hint of impatience, the surgeon turned away and pushed through the ward doors.

Sarah wondered at the persistence of his pursuit and struggled with a foolish inclination to be flattered by it as she hurried to the office to take the telephone call. She found Harriet Blake still seated at the desk, hand flying across forms.

'I've almost finished, Sister . . . '

Sarah nodded indifferently and reached for the telephone. Mr Bennett was an over-anxious husband who felt that his wife was being discharged too soon, and Sarah had to convince him that the removal of a benign ovarian cyst was not a major operation and that his wife was quite well enough to travel by car to her home that afternoon.

She hung up as Harriet capped her pen and began to marshal forms into a neat pile. 'Finds it inconvenient to have his wife home today, does he? He's probably enjoying a few days of freedom in typically male fashion.'

Sarah raised an eyebrow. 'You're a cynic, Miss Blake.'

The doctor shrugged. 'All men are opportunists, aren't they? I've never met one who isn't!'

For six years Sarah had thought much the same thing, but she didn't endorse the sentiment. In fact she was immediately indignant. Partly because she didn't like the blonde girl and partly because she had a strong sense of justice.

It was true that Patrick Egan had made the most of an opportunity when it offered, but hadn't she given him every encouragement at the time? And if Jeff's warm and friendly interest was opportunist . . . Well, it was very welcome balm for a badly bruised heart and pride, and she wished that she'd met him long before. Then she might not have earned a reputation as Sister Sour and Sister Stuffy, she thought bitterly, the echo of the surgeon's deep voice as he drawled the mocking epithets still rankling.

She was indignant on Mr Bennett's behalf, too. 'I think he's genuinely concerned about his wife,' she said stiffly. 'They seem to be a very devoted couple. I advise you not to say such things in front of the patients, Miss Blake. Most women are born worriers and setbacks can follow from that kind of anxiety about their husbands. They need to feel that they are badly missed, and it doesn't do a woman any good to wonder if her husband is enjoying a fling with someone else while she's out of the way!'

If Harriet felt the sting of the rebuke, it didn't show in the cool smile. 'I'm the soul of discretion,' she assured Sarah carelessly. 'You can trust me not to upset any of your patients, Sister.'

For some reason, Sarah didn't trust

her at all. From the first moment of meeting Harriet Blake, she'd felt that the girl would be a thorn in her side, some kind of a threat to her peace of mind . . .

7

Later in the week, Sarah left the ward to the care of Helen Champion while she attended the usual weekly conference of ward sisters presided over by Matron.

Nothing was actually said to her, but she was conscious of curious glances from her colleagues and a hint of disapproval and displeasure in Matron's manner, and she realised ruefully that gossip was circulating about herself and the new registrar.

Inevitably, their relationship had attracted the attention of her fellow nurses and his colleagues and the grapevine was buzzing with rumours. Sarah hoped they might convince Patrick Egan that she wasn't interested in him or likely to respond to his astonishing pursuit of her. Snubs and rebuffs seemed to have made almost no impression on him!

Coming out of Matron's office, she saw Liz, the theatre sister who was a friend from training days, and paused to speak. They talked to each other almost every day on the telephone with regard to patients, but it was some time since they'd seen each other, on or off duty.

As expected, Liz soon brought up the subject of the new member of the surgical staff. 'I wish you'd keep your friends informed of developments,' she said in light-hearted reproach. 'Everyone expects me to know all about your romance with Jeff Wyman and I can't tell them anything!'

'If and when it happens, you'll be the first to know,' Sarah promised, smiling.

Liz raised an amused eyebrow. 'My dear girl, don't you know that you're virtually engaged to the man and that he only came to Hartlake to be near you!'

'I'm glad you told me. One likes to know these things,' Sarah's sigh was a mixture of amusement and exasperation. 'Were *our* heads filled with such romantic nonsense about sisters and surgeons when we were student nurses, Liz? I'm sure we had far too much to do and too much to think about to bother with their love lives! We scarcely had time for our own! Today's juniors are so inventive and so imaginative that I wonder why they come into nursing when they might be writing romantic novels!'

Liz chuckled. 'So it's pure invention? You aren't involved with the handsome young surgeon? I must admit that I wondered if red hair was proving to be your downfall at last!' Her tone was teasing but there was curiosity and a degree of disappointment behind the light words.

'I like him, certainly. He's taken me out a few times,' Sarah said carefully, knowing that there was no point in denying something that was probably common knowledge among her fellow nurses. 'But that's all there is to it . . .'

'He hasn't been at Hartlake more than ten days or so, has he? Yet he's taken you out 'a few times' already? I call that very promising! I shall dust off my best hat just in case I'm invited to a wedding in the near future!'

'Oh, you're as bad as the juniors,' Sarah scolded. 'You know that I'd tell you if there was any truth in the gossip, Liz. There isn't — and I'll be grateful if you'll stamp on the rumours whenever you can!'

'I'll do my best,' Liz promised. 'But I'm really beginning to despair of you, Sarah. You can't want to end up as a lonely old maid and you're wasting all your opportunities!' Knowing her so well and for so long, Liz had thought it unlikely that her friend had plunged into a serious affair with a newcomer. But she was disappointed. Being a warm-hearted romantic, she liked to pair off all her friends and colleagues into happy couples, and it often troubled her that Sarah seemed to lead such a lonely and detached life away from the hospital. She was a lovely girl with a lot to offer any man, and it was puzzling that she kept them all so severely at arm's length.

'I wish you'd stop trying to marry me off, Liz. Whoever heard of a married Matron here at Hartlake?'

'I expect you'd make a marvellous Matron,' Liz retorted generously. 'But I'd still rather see you married to some nice man. I've one or two up my sleeve who might do for you, in fact. Come round for a meal and a comfortable gossip one evening and I'll tell you about them. Tomorrow night, if that suits? We haven't had a get-together in weeks!'

'Tomorrow night will be fine and I'd love to come — but only if you promise to keep your eligible bachelors up your sleeve and don't spring them on me,' Sarah said firmly. 'I know the way your devious mind works, remember!'

The girls went their separate ways on the words, Liz going back to Theatres and Sarah making her way to Mallory, thinking ruefully that she seemed to be the subject of more concern among her colleagues in the space of one short week than in all her years at Hartlake.

Liz meant well and she could forgive her kindly and affectionate efforts at matchmaking. Experience had taught her how to handle them. But she was ready to jump on anyone else who hinted by word or glance or giggle that there was anything romantic in her relationship with the new registrar — junior nurse, fellow Sister or even Matron!

For one thing, it was much too soon. For another, Sarah didn't feel that their relationship was meant to turn into real and lasting involvement. Her liking for Jeff Wyman increased with each day that passed and the more she saw of him, on and off the ward. Entirely at her ease with the young surgeon, she was renewing the youthful and very feminine delight in a man's admiration and attentions that had been cut short by that disastrous experience with Patrick Egan. She was discovering that it was possible to trust, and therefore might even be possible to love, without the fear of heartache and humiliation. Jeff's light touch promised to heal the still-throbbing wounds of the past.

But it couldn't coax her into giving all that he obviously wished. Her body seemed to shrivel at the merest hint of sexual longing in his kiss, his touch, his tone. She turned to ice in his arms and there was nothing she could do about an instinctive reluctance that sprang from too-eager and deeply-regretted surrender to another man, six years earlier.

She couldn't explain that to Jeff, of course. He assumed that it was merely virginal reluctance and apprehension that he would eventually overcome with patience and understanding and tender persuasion. No one but herself and Patrick Egan knew that she'd lost her virginity on a long-ago night — and *he* had forgotten.

Sarah wondered how long it would be before Jeff lost patience and interest and turned to another woman to satisfy his needs. There were plenty of girls waiting to step into her shoes, she realised. He was good-looking and personable and popular, a light-hearted and endearing flirt.

Many of her fellow nurses were casting out lures in his direction. So was Harriet Blake, who seemed ready to take him if she couldn't get her very attractive boss — or both of them, if she could manage it, Sarah thought dryly.

But even the thought of losing Jeff to her or someone else couldn't sweep Sarah willingly into his eager arms. They were good friends and she wanted to keep it that way, she told herself firmly, walking into the ward to find him there, sitting on the side of Mrs Spender's bed and flirting with the eighty-three-year-old patient whose wrinkled nutmeg face was wreathed in smiles in response to his obviously outrageous compliments.

The old lady was probably feeling like a girl again for those few minutes, and no doubt it would do her the world of good, Sarah thought tolerantly, smiling at patient and surgeon with swift, spontaneous warmth as she made her way along the ward to the office.

Jeff's approach might be unconventional and slightly too casual at times, flouting all the rules and regulations of traditional ward etiquette, but he was a tonic for the sick women on Mallory, who visibly brightened when he walked into the ward with his cheerful grin and cheeky banter. The nurses welcomed his visits, too, for his harmless flirtatiousness and mischievous sense of fun relieved the monotony of routine rounds and the slight heaviness of spirits that could attach to working on a surgical ward and nursing the seriously ill and the suffering.

With her thoughts on Jeff, Sarah pushed open the door of her office — and then her heart gave an odd little flip of delight at the sight of Patrick Egan.

He stood at the window that overlooked the ward, tall and brooding and darkly handsome, hands thrust into the pockets of his long white coat.

'Oh . . . Mr Egan!' The exclamation was involuntary and she was slightly annoyed with herself, hoping that it hadn't betrayed that absurd pleasure as well as surprise. But she hadn't expected to see him on the ward that morning.

Patrick turned. He'd watched her as she walked between the rows of beds, and seen the smile that she'd bestowed on Wyman. A smile that seemed to confirm all the wild rumours that were flying about the hospital and twisted a knife in his increasingly anxious heart.

'I wish I knew the secret of his success,' he drawled without the courtesy of a greeting, an edge to the deep voice. 'He seems to have won the heart of every woman in the place — from the newest Pet out of Training School to ward sisters who ought to know better!'

It was so pointed that a little warmth stole into her face. 'Mr Wyman?' she queried pleasantly, knowing perfectly well that the brusque words referred to the junior surgeon and that Patrick was possibly the only person at Hartlake who didn't like Jeff. She refused to be flattered by the implication. 'He's genuinely interested in people and goes out of his way to show that he cares about them and to please them. It isn't surprising that he's so well liked when he has such a warm heart and so much good nature.'

The surgeon raised a sardonic eyebrow and a mocking half-smile glinted in the dark eyes as he looked down at her. 'That's a glowing reference for a man you never knew until he came to Hartlake. It must have been love at first sight, but that seems rather out of character for the cool and level-headed Sister Sensible.'

Sarah looked at him coldly and

with dislike. The sarcastic devil seemed to delight in finding new names for her, she thought crossly — and not one of them was complimentary. Sour, stubborn and sensible! Each epithet pricked her like a barb in the flesh. Any girl would resent such a description of herself, she felt — and particularly when it sprang from a refusal to fall into arms that would only hold her briefly and much too casually and then put her aside as indifferently as before.

She moved to put the barrier of the desk between them as a *frisson* of awareness rippled down her unsuspecting spine, despite her determination to ignore his physical magnetism.

'I gather that you wished to see me,' she said crisply, all starch, the brisk manner rebuking him for introducing a personal note into their professional dealings. 'What can I do for you?'

'You could give me one of the smiles that you seem to keep for everyone else instead of freezing me to death,' he returned with a hint of impatience. 'All that ice makes it very difficult to get through to you, Sarah.'

'Are you here on ward business or merely to waste my time, Mr Egan? Because I'm very busy . . . ' Crushing him with the deliberate formality of address and the lack of warmth in her eyes or voice, Sarah sat down at the desk and reached for the pile of patients' folders that she'd already dealt with that morning with her usual efficiency.

He took the chair that faced her and crossed one long leg over the other as if he was settling for a lengthy stay. She looked at him with a tightening of her mouth and pointedly opened the first of the folders, unclipping her pen from the bib of her apron. She began to study details that she knew perfectly well, hoping that if she seemed to be engrossed in paperwork he would take the hint and depart.

For a few moments, Patrick regarded her with thoughtful eyes, wondering just how involved she was with his new assistant registrar. She seemed to be very much on the defensive. He'd heard some of the gossip that was circulating about them and none of it pleased him.

Doctors and nurses were constantly thrown together and they had a great deal in common, so perhaps it was inevitable that affairs should spring up between them occasionally. But they were usually discreet about such relationships and kept them outside their work and the hospital precincts. Wyman and Sarah appeared to be flaunting their interest in each other in a way that struck him as most unlike the responsible and reserved ward sister.

They met openly in the Kingfisher and the hospital social club, favourite haunts of Hartlake staff. Wyman had taken her to a show one evening and out for a meal on another night, and he was taking her to Founders Ball later that week as he'd been at pains to inform Patrick, obviously suspecting that he had an interest in Sarah. They seemed to snatch every opportunity for an exchange of meaningful smiles and glances or a private word, and Patrick had seen them strolling in the hospital gardens for a few moments of intimate togetherness in the midst of a busy day.

Inclined to blame Jeff Wyman for his own failure to make the slightest headway with the attractive Sarah Sweet, Patrick's jealousy and frustration were on the boil. Wanting her desperately, he could see her slipping through his unusually clumsy fingers and into the arms of another man, and there didn't seem to be anything he could do to prevent it.

'I came to have another go at persuading Mrs Spender to part with half her stomach, but it looks as if Wyman is saving me the time and trouble,' he broke the silence. Sarah looked up quickly. 'No doubt he's met with instant success, although it took weeks for her GP to persuade her to come in just for tests — and *you* know how resistant she's been to the very idea of surgery. He certainly seems to have a way with women.' He paused briefly. 'He's succeeded with you, too, I'm told,' he added with deliberate and faintly mocking implication.

The hot blood rushed into Sarah's face and her knuckles whitened as her fingers tightened fiercely on her pen. 'You've been misinformed,' she snapped, furious that malicious tongues were spreading such foul and utterly untrue rumours.

'Then he *isn't* taking you to the dance on Saturday?' he asked, all innocent surprise.

Sarah glowered, feeling foolish as she realised that he'd trapped her into leaping to exactly the kind of conclusion he'd intended — and learned what he wanted to know at the same time. 'Oh, *that* . . . ! Yes, he is, as a matter of fact,' she said coolly, almost defiantly, chin tilting and eyes sparkling with readiness to do battle.

Patrick shook his head in mock disapproval. 'It won't do, you know. A ward sister and a junior registrar! Matron won't like it. Nor do I. We shall have consultants turning up with first year nurses before we know where we are!'

'That wouldn't be the end of the world!' Sarah said tartly.

'Sir Henry would turn in his grave! Hartlake clings to its traditions and that helps to make it one of the finest hospitals in the world,' he reminded her smoothly. 'I really think that you'd better let *me* take you, Sarah. Much more the thing. Leave it to me! I'll explain to Wyman that he can't expect to enjoy a senior registrar's perks just because he fancies you.'

'I wish you'd go away and waste someone else's time with your nonsense,' she told him crossly. She closed the untouched folder, returned it to the pile and twisted the small silver watch on her breast to note the time. 'Mrs Bassett is due for an injection,' she said, relieved to have a valid excuse for escape. 'So if you don't mind . . . ' She rose with an air of dismissal.

Patrick got to his feet with a swift fluidity of movement that was surprising in a man of his impressive height and build. She looked up at him, wary and distrustful, and he smiled at her with sudden warmth.

'Do come with me, Sarah,' he said softly. 'I promise that it will be a night to remember . . . ' He slid his strong fingers over the slim hand that rested on the desk top as if she needed to steady herself before the onslaught of his overtures.

Sarah was foolishly flustered by the charm of that sudden smile, the persuasive warmth of his tone and the meaningful glow in his dark eyes that seemed to be threatening her heart as much as the senses that swirled for the merest touch of his hand. She was vividly conscious of the surgeon as he towered above her, tall and masculine and much too attractive for her peace of mind.

But the quiet, coaxing words were his mistake, for they saved her from yielding as they brought memories flooding to remind her of another night to remember, six years before.

She withdrew her hand. 'You haven't changed,' she said bitterly. 'Even the words you use are the same — and they still don't mean anything! You've said them too often and too many women have been stupid enough to believe your lies! You already gave me one night to remember, Patrick Egan — and I only wish I could forget it!'

Having nothing to say in defence of a crime that he still couldn't remember committing, Patrick put an arm about her, gathered her close and silenced her abruptly with the warm pressure of his mouth on her own.

For a brief, mad moment, Sarah delighted in the touch of his lips and the nearness of him, her whole body quivering and yearning with aching remembrance and renewed need. Then she broke free, shocked and shaken by her instant response to a potent sexuality that disregarded all her justifiable loathing and contempt for this man.

'Oh, you fool,' she said slowly, quietly, without passion. 'That could have cost both our jobs . . . '

She turned involuntarily to look through the window, but no one seemed to be taking any interest in what was happening in the office. Jeff was no longer sitting on the side of Mrs Spender's bed and the two nurses in sight were busy with the temps and blood pressure round. Sarah hoped with all her heart that no one had observed that compromising and very unprofessional kiss.

'I won't breathe a word to Matron as long as you make it worth my while,' Harriet Blake drawled from the doorway in cool, amused tones.

Sarah spun in obvious dismay. She

saw that for all the apparent amusement of the words, the amber eyes were hard and angry and calculating. Her heart sank. Of all the people who worked at Hartlake, she would have preferred any one of them, including Matron, to have witnessed the passionate kiss between surgeon and sister in the doubtful privacy of a ward office.

Patrick laughed, unruffled and seemingly unconcerned. 'Blackmail, eh?' he challenged lightly. 'What will it cost me? Lunch at the Kingfisher? Worth it to confound my colleagues who said I'd never get within kissing distance of Sarah Sweet!'

Sarah glanced at him, uncertain if he was merely making a quick recovery, thinking to protect her, or if there was more truth than she knew behind the careless words. It had been a foolish and dangerous thing for him to do, but he might have chanced it for a bet, she thought bitterly, realising the genuine amusement in those dancing dark eyes. She certainly wouldn't put anything past the despicable Patrick Egan! Dismayed, angry, she was unaccountably hurt, too . . .

'A pub lunch? You can do better than that, Patrick.' The blonde doctor smiled at him with unmistakable allure in the amber eyes. 'How about dinner at Mario's — on Saturday? Then, if you really want to seal my lips, you can take me to Founders Ball. I gather it's quite an event in the hospital year!'

'An excellent idea,' Patrick agreed promptly, wondering just how much of the conversation between himself and Sarah the girl had heard and if she was trying to manipulate the situation to her advantage. He didn't trust her not to cause trouble — for Sarah if not for himself — and if it should reach Matron's ears that a sister had allowed herself to be kissed by a surgeon within sight and sound of patients and nurses, she would be reprimanded and possibly suspended from a job that she obviously loved and did very well. 'But I seem to be getting the best of the bargain,' he added as though he was delighted to take Harriet out to dinner and then on to the traditional hospital dance.

Sarah walked to the door, scorn pulling her lips and glistening in the sapphire eyes. 'I think Miss Blake knows exactly what kind of a bargain she's making,' she said coldly, dismayed by his readiness to agree to the house officer's suggestion and marvelling that she'd been almost tempted to disappoint Jeff in order to accept a meaningless invitation from a man like Patrick Egan . . .

8

Having finally consented to surgery and signed the necessary forms, Mrs Spender was on Patrick's list for a partial gastrectomy the following morning.

Sarah arrived on the ward to learn that she'd already had her pre-med but was still apprehensive, and Audrey Crane reported that the old lady had spent a restless night.

'She's bound to be anxious, of course. I'm afraid she feels that she's been over-persuaded and now it's too late to change her mind. Very well, Staff. If you'll carry on with the washings, I'll go and have a chat to her. Any other problems?'

'Only Mrs Lomax.' The staff nurse laughed wryly. 'After making such a fuss about being in the main ward she now feels that it's much too lonely in a side ward and wants to move back. She complained of not feeling well in the night and no one bothering to look in to see if she was all right.'

'They did, of course?'

'I included her in my usual rounds and she was fast asleep each time. She just likes more than her fair share of attention, day *and* night.'

'She *is* difficult,' Sarah sympathised, having had several tussles with the demanding and querulous woman. 'She thinks we're all at her beck and call and should drop everything to answer her summons. I'm afraid I lost patience with her yesterday and told her that she should have gone private if she wanted preferential treatment.'

'She doesn't approve of private medicine.'

'So I gathered. I don't approve of private medicine either, and I don't expect any patient to be particularly grateful for anything we do, but I just wish that she'd bear in mind that I have twenty other patients on the ward who all merit just as much attention and concern as she does. Never mind! We're both used to dealing with people like Mrs Lomax, aren't we? I'll bring her back into the ward today and then we'll have her room for Mrs Spender when she comes down from Theatres. She won't be too well for a few days and she may need a special. I wanted a side ward for her and we didn't have one free, so in fact Mrs Lomax has done me a favour.'

'Don't let her hear you say so or she'll insist on staying where she is!' Audrey warned dryly.

Sarah made her way along the ward, exchanging smiles and greetings with the patients and nurses. Mrs Spender was drowsy but troubled, and she sat beside the bed, reassuring her and trying to straighten out some confusion in the old lady's mind. Finally, she promised to accompany her when she went to the theatre.

It was only on rare occasions that she visited Theatres these days. Escorting patients was a job that was usually assigned to a junior nurse. But she was at Mrs Spender's side when the porters arrived and she helped to transfer her from bed to theatre trolley and then held her hand all the way from the ward to the top floor of the hospital, where the operating theatres were situated, although patients always spoke of 'going down' for surgery and were seldom contradicted.

The department was a hive of activity, as usual. The surgeons and technicians and orderlies were busy with the preparations for the day's lists, hurrying or preoccupied figures in green trousers and tunics and caps, some masked and others with their masks dangling about their necks by the tapes. Porters bustled to and fro with the clearly-marked cylinders of oxygen and nitrous oxide and cyclopropane and carbon dioxide, all of different colours so that no mistakes were possible when they were connected.

There were several self-contained

units with ante-rooms, scrub annexes and changing-rooms, and each was the responsibility of an experienced sister or staff nurse. Liz was acting as scrub nurse for Patrick Egan that morning and it was her job to ensure that the theatre he was using was clean and sterile and ready for use and that her team of nurses knew exactly what to do and how to do it.

Mrs Spender was taken into the ante-room where the anaesthetist was waiting with a reassuring smile, a friendly word and the hypodermic injection that sent her off to sleep within seconds.

'Staying to watch, Sister?' he asked with a smile of belated surprise as he recognised Sarah. 'It promises to be an interesting case, apparently.'

'Oh, I don't think so,' she demurred. But she knew that the ward was in capable hands and she felt almost nostalgic for the days when she'd worked in Theatres as a third-year nurse. Unlike Liz, she hadn't seen it as her *métier*, but she'd enjoyed the work with its sense of urgency and drama and its constant variety and she'd liked the informal friendliness between members of the theatre staff that was seldom found on the wards.

Mrs Spender was wheeled into the operating-room and transferred to the table, carefully positioned by Liz and another nurse while the anaesthetist went to his place among the complicated array of valves and tubing and cylinders to begin the task of monitoring the patient whose life would be in his responsible and very skilled hands throughout the operation.

Through the round window in the swing door, Sarah saw Patrick enter the operating-room from the scrub annexe, gowned and gloved, all of his dark hair concealed by the theatre cap. He spoke to one of the theatre nurses as he entered and Sarah saw the swift gleam of feminine satisfaction in the girl's eyes as she smiled back at him. She hadn't seen or spoken to him since he'd kissed her in the ward office.

She lingered in the ante-room for a few more minutes while Patrick talked to his team, probably outlining the procedure he intended to follow, and waited for the anaesthetist to give him the go-ahead to begin operating. He was half turned towards Sarah, so that she received the benefit of his very handsome profile with the strong nose and the intelligent sweep of brow.

Studying him with reluctant but honestly admitted admiration, she felt the tug of attraction and the stirring of excitement as she thought of the way he'd kissed her, with as much tenderness as passion in the seeking of his warm lips and the encompassing embrace of his arms. On a sudden surge of absolute truth, she confessed to wanting him just as much now as she had all those years before. But she hoped she had too much sense and self-control to be swamped by that wanting all over again.

Belatedly, she realised that Jeff was also in the operating-room, red curls escaping from the cap to reveal his identity as he stood with his back to Sarah, listening intently and occasionally nodding agreement or understanding. He was not a small man by any means, but somehow he seemed almost insignificant beside the tall and powerful figure of the senior surgeon. Certainly Patrick Egan had the edge on his new registrar when it came to looks and physique and charisma. But Sarah told herself firmly that Jeff knocked spots off the surgeon when it came to character and integrity and real warmth of heart. She was beginning to admit the need of a man in her life, at last. Why shouldn't that man be Jeff? Only a fool would think of opening her arms to someone like Patrick Egan for a second time!

Suddenly, the surgeon turned, as if he sensed her presence and her scrutiny. He looked at her so briefly that she was irritated by the sweeping indifference of his glance. But he said something to Liz and almost immediately a nurse hurried out of the theatre to push open the swing door of the ante-room.

'Would you care to scrub up and watch, Sister? Mr Egan thinks you might be interested and he has no objection,' she declared with her warm smile.

'He's very kind, but I don't know if I can spare so much time,' Sarah said carefully. 'I ought to get back to Mallory . . .'

'It shouldn't be a lengthy op. He's a very fast worker — and a fascinating one,' the nurse encouraged.

'Yes, I know . . .' In more ways than one, Sarah thought dryly, but she was careful to keep all hint of animosity out of her tone. Her hesitation was shortlived. She was absurdly pleased that he'd issued the invitation and she decided to accept it. 'It *is* one of our quieter days on the ward and Mrs Spender happens to be a favourite with me. I could ring down and tell my staff nurse to carry on without me . . .'

'Do — and then hurry up and

change into a theatre frock. Mr Egan won't wait for you, of course. But you shouldn't miss any of the interesting surgery . . . '

As a spectator, Sarah didn't need to scrub up with the routine thoroughness of the theatre team. She wouldn't be handling instruments or passing swabs and the surgeons and scrub nurse would be standing between her and the operating-table.

She put on sterile gown and cap and mask and changed black, low-heeled brogues for theatre slippers and went quietly into the operating-room as Patrick cut down into the peritoneum with confident skill.

He didn't glance up as she slipped into a position that gave her a splendid view of the table and the laid-up trolley with its gleaming instruments and the draped figure of the patient. He didn't speak, too intent on what he was doing. But Sarah knew that he'd registered her entrance into the theatre.

Jeff turned to nod at her in a warm

and friendly welcome that was reflected in his grey eyes — and was promptly rebuked for a momentary inattention by Patrick as his grip on a retractor slackened slightly. He muttered a hasty apology.

Watching, Sarah was fascinated. Patrick's gloved hands were swift and very sure, but he was much more than a clever technician, she thought admiringly, as he cut and clamped, separated tissue and removed the diseased section of the duodenum. Despite the clinical conditions and aseptic surroundings, the caring and concern for his patient showed through, she felt. She'd heard that he was good. It was a pleasure to watch him at work.

His concentration on the very demanding surgery was complete. He seemed oblivious to everything and everyone but the patient on the table, the anaesthetist who provided him with constant and comprehensive reports on her condition, the surgeon who assisted him by applying clamps,

177

holding retractors, inserting suction tubes and sealing off bleeders with the diathermy needle, and the extremely efficient Liz, who anticipated his every need and supplied it so promptly that she seemed to be an extension of his fast-moving and clever hands.

They were an excellent team who were well used to working with each other on such delicate surgery, and it seemed that Jeff had slotted neatly into place since his arrival at Hartlake.

At last, sooner than Sarah had thought possible, Patrick moved back from his position at the table and Jeff moved forward to set the final sutures in place. Sweat glistened on the surgeon's brow but there was a glow of satisfaction in the deep-set dark eyes and an obvious relaxing of tension in the powerful frame.

'She'll do,' he said quietly, using the traditional term that predicted full return to health for his patient, and no one in that room doubted the prognosis.

Patrick Egan knew his job thoroughly and well and he was expected to step into Sir Lionel's shoes in the fullness of time. He was clever and dedicated and obviously ambitious. Sarah, impressed and admiring, was almost ready in that moment to forgive the man anything because of his undeniable ability and brilliance as a surgeon.

He turned to her and looked directly into her eyes, smiling with sudden and enchanting warmth that held as much intimacy as if they were alone in the room. Her heart lurched with an emotion that she thought she'd overcome long before he came back to Hartlake. Flustered and dismayed, she lowered the veil of thick, long lashes before that compelling gaze, afraid of what he might read in her too-expressive eyes, hastily rejecting the absurdity that a man she had reason to dislike and distrust might be a man she could love, after all.

She realised abruptly that he'd turned to her for a word or a smile of approval. Conscious that he was waiting expectantly, she rushed into speech. 'Well done . . . a very neat piece of work, Mr Egan!' she said brightly, and realised too late that her tone had been condescending and supercilious. The warmth of dismay swept into her face as Jeff turned to look at her in obvious surprise and a hint of indignation on Patrick's behalf, and Liz looked from her to the surgeon with mingled amusement and curiosity in her brown eyes.

Patrick's expression hardened. Then he executed a sardonic bow and walked out of the operating-room without another word, drawing off mask and gloves and dropping them with an air of finality into the 'dirty' bin in passing. Affront was evident in the set of his dark head, the rigidity of his broad back and the stalk of his stride.

Sarah looked after him with a sinking heart and contrition in her dark blue eyes as she realised that the hasty and unthinking words might have seemed like one snub too many to a proud man.

'Oh dear,' she murmured wryly as the swinging door of the scrub annexe cut the surgeon from view. 'I'm afraid that wasn't well received . . .'

'Scarcely surprising, is it?' Jeff's quiet tone held the hint of rebuke, for he had a great deal of admiration for his new boss, even if he was suspicious of the surgeon's interest in Sarah that might be a threat to his own hopes. ''Neat' as a description of my surgical skill is not one that I'd welcome, either, frankly.' He didn't add *'from a mere nurse'*, but the words hung on the air, not needing to be spoken to make Sarah feel even more uncomfortable. 'Damned with faint praise, as they say,' he went on dryly. Then his grey eyes suddenly twinkled at her above his mask as he relented. *'Brilliant* or *breathtaking* would do very nicely, however.'

'He doesn't need me to tell him that he's wonderful when everyone else is gasping with admiration,' Sarah said defensively.

Jeff raised a surprised eyebrow. 'He doesn't need anyone to tell him that he's good. He knows it. But none of us are averse to the occasional word of praise for a job well done from someone who knows that it isn't as easy as it looks in experienced hands.'

Liz frowned at them both, warning them that her nurses were all ears, although they pretended not to be aware of the exchange as they counted swabs and checked instruments and hovered to do her bidding. Jeff took the hint and went on with the task of sewing-up.

Very soon, Liz was dressing the wound while the anaesthetist began to adjust valves and turn taps, preparing the patient for a gradual return to consciousness in the recovery room.

Sarah removed her gown and mask as soon as Mrs Spender had been wheeled out of the room. 'Time I was getting back to the ward,' she said lightly, smiling at Liz. 'Thanks for the entertainment.'

'Glad you enjoyed the show. Come again!'

'If I'm invited,' Sarah said wryly.

'I suggest you go and make your peace with Patrick before you leave Theatres. We have to work with him for the rest of the day!'

The twinkle in the warm brown eyes told Sarah that the theatre sister didn't regard the surgeon as any kind of tyrant and that they were very good friends. She felt an odd little pang that was almost envy of their obviously uncomplicated liking for each other.

'I don't know why he took offence. I paid him a compliment, I thought,' she said lightly as though it was all very unimportant.

'Oh, the words were all right. It was the way you said them,' Liz told her. 'Just as if you were praising a very new Pet for a neat piece of bandaging. Very Sister Tutor! Fortunately, he has a forgiving nature. I dare say he'll speak to you again. Thousands wouldn't! Sir Lionel would have wiped the floor with you and banned you from Theatres for the rest of your time at Hartlake!' Her gaze rested on Sarah's slightly flushed face and strangely defensive eyes. 'I'm not probing, but don't you like our Patrick?' she asked gently.

'Must I like him? That famous charm doesn't cut any ice with me, Liz. I've known him too long.'

'Don't tell me that you didn't fancy him in the distant days of our youth,' Liz mocked merrily. 'We all did!'

Sarah shrugged. 'We all pretended that we did,' she amended. 'It was the fashion to sigh over Patrick Egan. But he wasn't my type in those days and he isn't now. I must dash! I'll see you this evening — about eight!'

She hurried away, wondering if she would ever convince her romantic friend that she was indifferent to Patrick Egan's good looks and practised charm. It was becoming increasingly difficult to convince herself, she admitted wryly.

Some minutes later, she emerged from the nurses' changing room to the constant bustle of trundling trolleys and preoccupied staff, muted voices and the clatter of instruments, and everywhere permeated with the distinctive smells of ether and antiseptic. Theatres meant drama and excitement but Sarah felt that she preferred the comparative peace and quiet of a busy surgical ward.

As she passed the surgeons' sitting-room, she glanced through the open doorway to see Patrick pouring coffee, his hands dealing as deftly with the task as they had so recently dealt with the business of improving the quality of life for an old lady. She stopped short on a sudden impulse to speak to him, to try to make amends for an obviously offensive tone.

Patrick turned, the dark blue dress that was so distinctive in a place where everyone wore theatre greens catching his eye. He looked at the slender girl, dark hair gleaming in its neat coil, a slightly anxious expression in the sapphire eyes and the delicate features of her lovely face invoking an increasingly familiar tug at his heart despite the still-smarting irritation.

For a moment they looked at each other in silent challenge. Sarah saw that there wasn't the trace of a smile or the hint of any warmth in his uncompromising stare and she experienced an unreasonable panic that she might have alienated him completely.

She rushed impulsively into speech. 'Patrick, I'm sorry! That sounded quite dreadful and it really wasn't what I meant to say!'

'You *didn't* feel that it was a neat piece of work?' It was dry, slightly mocking. He was careful not to show his pleasure at that impulsive and apparently unconscious use of his first name. It seemed to prove that she thought of him as *Patrick* and only kept him at a deliberate distance with the formal *Mr Egan*, he decided with

186

a glow of satisfaction.

'Of course it was — but so much more. You're a very fine surgeon. Everyone says so, but I hadn't seen you operate before and I was most impressed.' It was slightly breathless, the generous words imbued with sincerity and much more warmth than she usually had for him.

'Praise from Sister Sweet,' he commented with the sardonic lift of an eyebrow. 'All the sweeter for being so rare. It's usually all kicks and no kudos.'

'I hope I haven't made any secret of my admiration for your work and your caring attitude to the patients,' she said stiffly.

'My admiration for you isn't limited to your ability as a ward sister,' he drawled. 'I don't forget that you're a woman as well as a nurse, whereas you overlook the fact that I'm a man as well as a surgeon. I have feelings like everyone else and I object to being snubbed before an interested audience.'

Some of his anger was showing through the controlled manner and Sarah knew it was justified. At the same time, she bridled at the rebuke and the arrogant tone and remembered that she had a grievance of her own. Her chin shot up. 'And I object to being kissed before an interested audience!'

Patrick laughed, good humour abruptly restored, something deep within him responding instinctively to the spirited sparkle in the lovely eyes. 'I'm sorry about that. Oh, not that I kissed you. I don't regret that. Just the venue. It happened to be Harriet, but it might have been Matron or my boss or a patient. As you so rightly said, it could have cost both our jobs. As it is, it's cost me an evening with you. A high price to pay!'

It was too light to be convincing. Sarah's lip curled. 'I expect you'll have a much better time with Miss Blake,' she said coldly. 'You weren't taking me to the dance, in any case. I think I made that clear.'

'We could make it a foursome,' he mused, ignoring the snap of her words. 'That way we'll at least have a chance to dance together . . . '

'That *will* be the highlight of the evening!'

'You're right. It will.' Patrick smiled with a sudden, heart-stopping mix of tenderness and amusement.

Feeling that she trembled on the verge of a dangerous abyss, Sarah hastily drew back from the enchantment of the smile in those dark eyes.

'I haven't any wish to dance with you, Mr Egan. So don't bother to ask,' she said tartly.

She pretended not to hear the sound of Jeff's voice calling her name as she whisked along the corridor to the lift. She'd had quite enough of men for one morning, she thought crossly. Patrick Egan alone threatened to be too much for her to handle . . .

9

One swift, comprehensive glance about the ward assured Sarah that Helen Champion had coped perfectly well in her absence, and she had a warm smile and a few words of well-earned praise for the staff nurse who'd apparently taken to heart the scolding she'd earned a few days earlier.

She'd always liked the usually reliable and responsible nurse, and she was still inclined to blame Jeff for the disasters of that particular afternoon. For she observed that Helen usually hovered in the near vicinity of the registrar whenever he was on the ward and that Jeff usually managed to find time for a brief and mildly flirtatious exchange. Recalling that he'd paid the girl a fair amount of attention at his party, she felt that he'd encouraged Helen to believe that he was interested in her and then disappointed her with his obvious preference for a ward sister. Sarah was flattered and she liked the surgeon, but she was honest enough to admit that she was using him to some extent.

She went to talk to Mrs Lomax who had been moved back into the main ward at her own request. She was still finding fault with everyone and everything, but Sarah had learned in her training days that such irritability was often due to anxiety and discomfort. It was part of a nurse's care for a patient to find the cause of one and alleviate the other as much as possible. So she made a note on the chart that suggested a more effective analgesic to combat the pain and encourage mobility, and then spent some time in coaxing Mrs Lomax to confide her problems. Warming to the sympathy and concern in her smile and tone, Mrs Lomax was soon enlarging on the difficulties of running a business in the present economic climate and detailing the breakdown of her marriage, which was only one of the factors that had led to her perforated ulcer and emergency admission to Hartlake.

Sarah listened patiently and with understanding, knowing that the ward staff were going about their work under Helen's capable supervision, and eventually she came away from the patient's bedside knowing that her nurses would benefit from Mrs Lomax's more relaxed and much sweeter mood.

Mrs Spender was brought down from the recovery unit soon after and duly installed in the side ward. Sarah assigned one of the juniors to monitor her every half-hour and report immediately if she observed any respiratory or cardiovascular difficulties. Mrs Spender was a very old lady and she had undergone major surgery. It was essential to keep a careful eye on her condition over the next twenty-four hours.

Later that afternoon, Sarah was adjusting the flow of the saline drip attached to Mrs Spender's arm when Jeff came to check on the patient's condition. She had to suppress a tiny flicker of disappointment that he was standing in for his boss.

'How is she?' Jeff reached for the chart and glanced over the neat and careful entries. 'Fairly stable, I see . . . good! She's going to make it. She's a grand old girl with a marvellous constitution . . . ' He gave the chart to Sarah to return to its hook, and lifted the frail wrist to check the pulse. 'How do you feel, May?'

He raised his voice to penetrate the mists of semi-consciousness and used her first name because he knew that she preferred friendly familiarity to the formality that frightened her a little. Like so many of the old people in the neighbourhood, she'd been coming to Hartlake with her ills for most of her life, using the casualty department as if it was a doctor's surgery and regarding the young doctors who attended her as her local GP. She'd told Jeff at their first meeting that everyone knew her as May — and so she'd been May ever since to him and to some of the nurses on the ward.

The eyelids flickered at the sound of his voice. She looked very old and sunken without her teeth, but her eyes were an incredible baby blue beneath the crêpey lids and her wrinkled cheeks were as rosy as a young girl's from the anaesthetic and the drugs that were being carefully infiltrated into her system via the drip.

'Going down at last, am I? About time, too,' she said drowsily, her normally sharp intelligence and awareness disorientated by surgery.

'It's all over, love . . . you're back in the ward and looking great! We're all very pleased with you! I'll be taking you to the pictures in a few days, just as I said! Wait and see!'

As they left the side ward a few minutes later, Sarah smiled at the red-haired registrar with sudden sweetness. 'I think I'm jealous,' she declared lightly. 'I had no idea that you were making up to another girl behind my back!'

The grey eyes were suddenly wary. Jeff busied himself with tucking the tubing of his stethoscope neatly into the pocket of his white coat, carefully nonchalant and carefully not looking at Sarah.

'Oh, you know how it is! The ratio of nurses to unmarried doctors must be about thirty to one and it's the duty of each one of us to keep his quota as happy as possible! I have to share myself between you and a lot of other girls!' It was light and laughing, and not an entirely convincing attempt to counter an apparent accusation.

Sarah was slightly startled. But she made a quick recovery. 'I was talking about May, but it seems that you're unfaithful to her, too,' she countered brightly. 'I knew I could never compete with an eighty-three-year-old charmer who's already had three husbands and seems to be looking for a fourth! But

I'll fight tooth and nail to keep you out of the clutches of my nurses!'

Jeff grinned and put an arm about her waist. 'I'd rather have you than a dozen of your nurses,' he told her generously, almost meaning it. 'So it will probably be a straight fight between you and dear old May! As she's temporarily out of action, how about coming to the pictures with me this evening, Sarah?'

She frowned at him and side-stepped that embracing arm as a nurse emerged from the ward with a covered receiver and headed for the sluice. 'I can't make it tonight. I've a date.' She didn't add that she was spending the evening with Liz. It wouldn't do him any harm to wonder if she was seeing another man, she decided. She didn't doubt that he'd issue an invitation to someone else at the first opportunity. Probably Helen Champion.

Sarah wasn't really jealous. They were both free agents. She'd become fond of Jeff, but her emotions weren't as deeply involved as she almost wished.

For falling in love with him must surely protect her from making a fool of herself over Patrick Egan all over again — and that was a very real danger . . .

* * *

Sarah flumped into the deep cushions of the sofa, replete with good food and slightly light-headed from the wine that her friend had served with the supper. 'That was a fantastic meal!' she declared warmly, smiling at Liz as she followed her into the room with the coffee-tray.

'Well worth the mounds of washing-up?'

'Twice the washing-up! You really are a super cook, Liz. I can't understand why you haven't been snapped up by some discerning doctor in search of a wife.' It wasn't tactless. She knew that Liz was still single because she wanted it that way. There were plenty of men attracted by the warm heart and smiling good nature of the theatre sister.

Liz grinned, dispensing coffee. 'I was behind the door when good looks were handed round and that's the kind of thing that even discerning doctors seem to prefer to good cooking,' she returned lightly, understating her claim to prettiness in characteristic manner. 'Do you want cream?'

Sarah eyed the jug. 'I ought to be strong-minded enough to say no,' she said ruefully.

Liz liberally added cream and passed the cup of coffee across. 'What about you? Isn't it time that you gave up helping suffering humanity and helped yourself to some of the good things in life? Like a husband and a semi-detached and a handful of children.'

'More trouble than they're worth, I'm told. You should hear some of my patients on the subject of marriage. Not a good word to say for it until they hear that one of the juniors has got herself engaged, and then there isn't a dry eye in the place and they can't urge her to the altar fast enough. Fair shares of misery for all, I'm tempted to assume!'

'You're a cynic! Seriously, Sarah . . . '

Knowing what was coming, she didn't allow her well-meaning friend to continue. 'Seriously, Liz,' she mocked gently, laughing, 'I'm happy as I am. I don't want a husband. Not yet, anyway. When I do, I'll let you know and you can parade all your eligibles.' She stiffened as the doorbell cut across her words and shot a suspicious glance at Liz. 'That isn't one of them now, is it? Because even your *coq au vin* hasn't put me in the mood to appreciate your match-making efforts,' she warned.

'I haven't laid anything on. I won't say that I wasn't tempted, but knowing your views . . . ' Liz got to her feet. 'Probably just a neighbour wanting to borrow something.'

She was right. Patrick had come up from his ground-floor flat in the same house to ask for the loan of a corkscrew. The unmistakable sound of his deep velvet voice in the tiny hall set all Sarah's defences on alert before he followed Liz into the living-room. But he looked at her in such obvious surprise that she instantly acquitted her friend of conspiring with the surgeon.

'Sorry . . . I'm intruding!' Dark eyes lingered appreciatively on the slender girl in the coral silk frock, hair drawn back to cluster in a knot of curls on the nape of her neck. Patrick constantly marvelled that he'd been so blind in those first weeks on Mallory to the beauty of those delicately-sculpted features, the sparkling dark blue eyes and the gleaming mass of rich dark hair that framed a perfect oval face.

Sarah looked back at him coolly, meeting the blatant admiration of his gaze with assumed indifference in defiance of the way her heart quickened as he smiled a greeting. She nodded a rather chilly acknowledgement that was in marked contrast to the beam of welcome that Liz was bestowing on him.

'Of course you aren't!' Liz declared stoutly, the warmth of her tone and smile compensating for the block of ice sitting on her sofa. 'Stay for a while . . . unless you're entertaining?'

'No. I'm having a quiet evening with a couple of good books, actually.'

'And turning into a solitary drinker by the sound of it! How desperate!' Liz teased.

'The situation became desperate when I couldn't find a corkscrew. Jeremy borrowed mine the other night and didn't return it, and he isn't in at the moment. So I wondered if you'd come to the rescue.'

'I happen to have a spare one and you're very welcome to it,' she assured him. Then, ignoring Sarah's unsmiling silence and the probability of later reproach, she swept on in her usual friendly fashion. 'Sit down and have some coffee with us, Patrick . . . it's freshly-made. I'll just get another cup!'

She vanished into the kitchen.

After a moment's hesitation, he walked over to the sofa and sat down beside Sarah. She didn't actually draw away from him, but withdrawal was implied in the slight tensing of her frame and the way that she stubbornly refused to look at him.

A wry smile tugged at Patrick's lips. '*Am* I intruding?' he asked quietly.

She shrugged. 'It isn't my flat.'

'It seems to be your evening for a get-together with Liz. I don't want to spoil it for you, so just say the word if you'd rather I refused coffee and took myself off. But perhaps you were on the point of leaving,' he suggested. 'Isn't that what usually happens whenever our paths cross like this?'

'I was on the point of settling down to a pleasant evening with an old friend,' she told him. 'I see more than enough of you at the hospital.'

He leaned his dark head against the cushions and regarded her thoughtfully. 'You could look on me as an old friend, too, Sarah. We've known each other for a long time, after all.'

'Have we? I thought you were suffering from a loss of memory on that score!' It was quick and scathing.

'Ouch! Below the belt . . . ' he murmured ruefully, amusement glinting in the dark eyes as Liz came back from the kitchen, brandishing the required corkscrew and the extra cup.

She sat down to deal with the coffee-pot. 'This is nice, isn't it?' she said comfortably, apparently unaware of the atmosphere and the stony expression on Sarah's lovely face. 'Being together with no work to do and plenty of time to talk over old times . . . '

'I'm afraid I don't share your sentimental attitude towards the old times,' Sarah said brightly. 'There are lots of things about my early days at Hartlake that I'd sooner forget. The agonies of being a first-year, for instance. Chivvied by irate sisters and chased by over-amorous doctors and making stupid mistakes on and off the wards.'

'That sounds more like me than you,' Liz declared. 'I can't believe you ever made mistakes, on or off the wards. You sailed through exams and were the apple of every sister's eye — and even made Nurse of the Year! The really dedicated type, staying in with your books while the rest of us ran wild with the med students, knowing all the answers while we bluffed our way through and hoped that none of the patients died as a result!'

She exaggerated wildly, humorously. But it had been rather like that, Sarah thought wryly. 'You make me sound thoroughly obnoxious!' she protested.

'So you were!' The twinkle in the warm brown eyes belied the ready retort. 'A born nurse, according to Sister Tutor — and held up almost daily as an example of the perfection we should all strive to attain.'

'The most popular girl in the Training School,' Patrick drawled, a sardonic lift to an eyebrow.

Sarah smiled frostily.

'She didn't deserve to be. But she was, oddly enough.' Liz grinned. 'You've always had a lovely nature, haven't you, Sarah?'

'My first-years wouldn't agree with you,' she retorted. 'You seem to have forgotten what they call me!'

'Cheeky imps! But it was only to be expected with a name like Sweet, I suppose. It must have been an irresistible temptation to parody it. But you know the remedy, Sarah. Change it!' There was meaningful mischief in the light words and laughing glance.

'Oh, I don't mind the infants,' Sarah said coolly. 'It's when grown men play the same silly game that I lose patience.' She didn't look at Patrick as she spoke, but the inference was unmistakable.

Liz glanced from sister to surgeon with an amused and speculative gleam in her brown eyes. Then she got to her feet. 'I've just remembered that

I promised to ring my mother this evening. She hasn't been too well lately. Do you mind entertaining each other for a few minutes while I make a quick call . . . ?'

There was a public telephone on the landing outside the flat and she closed the door behind her. Left alone with Patrick Egan, Sarah was visibly annoyed. It was too bad of Liz to be so blatant in her efforts to throw them together, she thought crossly. She leaned forward and set down her empty coffee-cup on the tray with a little tremble of her hand that caused it to chink in the saucer. She was much too aware of the attractive man at her side and she suspected that he knew it.

Patrick smiled reassuringly. 'Relax,' he said. 'I'm not going to cry *alone at last!*' and throw myself on you.'

She looked at him coldly, unamused. 'Can I depend on that?'

He shook his dark head, mischief dawning in the deep-set eyes that crinkled so endearingly when he smiled.

'No,' he admitted cheerfully. 'Don't trust me at all, Sarah. You're a very exasperating girl. As you insist on keeping me at arm's length I'm forced to take my opportunies whenever and wherever I can, and this seems an irresistible one, I'm afraid.'

Sarah didn't smile and she was determined not to show that she was disarmed by the flattering warmth of the words. 'Why can't you simply take no for an answer?' she demanded coolly.

He looked at her, suddenly serious. 'I want you too much.'

She bit her lip. The quiet words were convincing and her heart unexpectedly shook in response to the look in his eyes and the meaning in his deep voice. She reminded herself hastily that his desire for her meant very little and had already led to disaster in the past. Surely she wasn't such a fool as to be tempted all over again by this man's looks and charm and physical magnetism — his velvet tongue and caressing smile and the breath-taking promise of delight in the dark eyes?

'I've heard it all before,' she said with scorn. 'And I'm not impressed!'

'You're not giving me a chance to impress you.' He laid an arm lightly along the back of the sofa, long fingers just brushing the nape of her neck to send a tremor of quivering excitement rippling down her sensitive spine. 'You're still judging me on the strength of something that happened when I was an irresponsible and rather wild young medical student. I'm a very different person these days, believe me.'

'I don't think you've changed at all — except that you seem to prefer sisters and staff nurses to unsuspecting first-year nurses these days!' He'd been a houseman and not a medical student when they'd met on that memorable night, but she didn't bother to correct him. It was merely further proof, if she'd needed it, that he didn't remember anything at all about it! Impatiently, she shrugged his tentative, too-disturbing touch from her neck.

Patrick sighed. 'I'm not getting through to you, am I?' He twined his fingers in her soft, thick curls and leaned to kiss her with a different kind of persuasion in mind.

His lips had scarcely brushed her cheek on the way to her mouth before she'd thrust him away with angry hands against his powerful chest, alarmed by the potency in his nearness and her own leaping response to it. 'You don't seem to know anything but body language!' she said tartly.

His arm came down about her shoulders to imprison her firmly as she tried to get up from the sofa. 'You refuse to listen to anything else,' he told her softly and kissed her with determined lips.

For the merest of moments, Sarah's own lips warmed and parted and began to hunger in response to the kiss that fanned the flickering flame of her desire for this man to soaring, searing heights. With an effort she resisted him, and her hands flew to grasp his crisp black curls

209

and tug at them angrily, forcing him to lift his head on an 'ouch' of annoyance and pain.

Abruptly, he let her go, angry in his turn.

Sarah glowered at him. 'Now will you believe that I'm not interested?'

Patrick sat back with a shrug of his broad shoulders, but his eyes smouldered. 'Have it your way! I'm not forcing myself on a woman who starts to shake as soon as I get too close. What the hell is it with you, anyway? Are you really an iceberg — or is it just me?'

He didn't really think that she was frigid. Briefly but reassuringly, he'd sensed her response to the sexuality that had always won him any woman he wanted. He'd sensed her rising panic, too. Was she so afraid of his passion — and why?

However it was, it seemed that he would need all his patience and all his powers of persuasion to overcome her doubt and distrust. If he didn't want her so much and feel so strongly that they were right for each other, he'd have given up the pursuit by this time, he thought wearily.

Sarah didn't answer him. She got to her feet trembling, thankful that he didn't seem to know that her treacherous body quickened at his merest touch and burst into fierce flame when he gathered her into his arms.

She crossed the room to stare unseeingly at Liz's prized collection of porcelain miniatures in a glass-fronted cabinet, needing to put as much space as possible between herself and the surgeon. Silent and shaken, she struggled with the mix of emotions that he always managed to evoke in her heart and body.

Patrick studied her, hands locked between his knees, eyes narrowed. He saw the troubled rise and fall of her small breasts beneath the thin silk of her frock, the heavy throb of the pulse in her slender throat and the disquiet in the lovely face, and wished he understood the tumult and the tension that kept him at bay.

The loud slam of the front door and the sound of singing announced that Liz had returned from the telephone. Sarah turned to snatch up the coffee-tray and hurry with it into the kitchen . . .

Liz meant well, but she was almost too tactful at times, she thought crossly, running water and clattering cups.

She couldn't hear the excuse that Patrick offered for leaving so soon and so suddenly, but she was relieved when he called a brisk and carefully non-committal good night to her on his way from the flat.

She didn't make any reply. She saw no reason to pretend that they were on good terms just to please her sentimental friend. Heaven knew why Liz wanted to push them into each other's arms when it must be obvious that they were totally unsuited.

As if the Hartlake Heart-Throb and Sister Sour could ever be a pair!

10

Liz joined Sarah in the kitchen, agog with curiosity and trying to conceal it, convinced that something had happened between the sister and the surgeon while she had been out of the flat. His abrupt departure and the set expression on Sarah's face told her that it had been a mistake to try to help matters along.

'You could have left those,' she said lightly, reaching for a tea-cloth to dry the cups that Sarah had stacked on the drainer. 'I thought Patrick meant to stay for a while, but I guess he was bored by our girlish reminiscences.' She tossed it into the air, carefully casual.

Undeceived, Sarah turned to look at her friend. 'He left because I don't want him in my life and I'd just told him so for about the tenth time,' she said levelly, as though it had been an utterly unimportant exchange. A man making a pass and a girl rejecting it and nothing more than that. She wished it was that simple!

'Then he *does* fancy you!' Liz was delighted to discover that her usually reliable instinct hadn't been at fault. 'Are you really not interested, Sarah?' she asked curiously. 'He's so nice!'

'I'm not playing hard to get, if that's what you mean!' It was sharp. 'Don't put that idea into his head, for heaven's sake! I don't think he's so nice. I've no time for men like Patrick Egan!'

'I suppose you'll bite my head off if I dare to suggest that you'd do well to see more of Patrick and less of Jeff Wyman,' Liz ventured, feeling that they'd been friends for long enough for her to tread on obviously dangerous ground.

She had always been fond of Sarah and concerned about the lack of meaningful relationships in her life, and she wasn't at all happy about the sudden and uncharacteristic affair with the new registrar. Sarah had always been wary of forming friendships with members of the staff, and Liz was shrewd enough to wonder if a public display of interest in one man was meant to camouflage a much warmer and very private interest in another.

'Oh, you've been listening to the gossip about him,' Sarah said dismissively. 'I know he flirts, but I'm not too serious about Jeff, you know. I like him and he likes me and we don't make too many demands on each other. I don't expect to be the only girl in his life.'

'That's just as well,' Liz said dryly. 'It seems there's a girl at his previous hospital who thought she *was* the only girl in his life and then found that he was involved with a married staff nurse and playing fast and loose with half a dozen others.'

'Jeff!' Sarah laughed and shook her head. 'He may be a flirt but he isn't a fool. He wouldn't risk his job or his professional reputation for any girl. There *was* a girl who wanted to marry him and she tried to make trouble when he ended the affair by spreading malicious rumours about him. That kind of mud has a way of sticking, unfortunately — and we both know how careful doctors have to be! In fact she made things so difficult that he applied for the job at Hartlake to get away from her and all the talk.'

'That's the gospel according to St Jeffery, I suppose?'

Sarah glanced at her friend, frowning. It was so sceptical and so unexpectedly tart for someone usually so good-natured that she was prone to think well of everyone. 'I'm not saying that he's a saint. I just think he's telling the truth. But you don't, obviously. Why not? What do you have against him? He's so nice!' she added, gently teasing as she turned the tables.

Liz shrugged. 'Feminine intuition, that's all. He's amusing and clever and very easy to like, but I don't trust him. He probably doesn't mean any harm but he's the type to say or do whatever suits the moment, either to please or to get what he wants.' She hesitated briefly. 'I don't mean to interfere, but there haven't been too many men in your life, Sarah,' she said as tactfully as she could. 'I don't want to see you get hurt by falling for the wrong kind of man.'

'And you think I'd be safe with Patrick Egan!' Sarah laughed scornfully and swept a strand of dark hair from her face with an impatient hand. 'Now there *is* a man who doesn't hesitate to say whatever suits the moment to get what he wants!' she declared bitterly. 'Any girl fool enough to trust *him* is just asking for trouble — and I do know what I'm talking about! I know you mean well, Liz. But I'm not as naive or as gullible as you think I am. I'm not in any danger of losing my head or my heart, much as I like Jeff. But if I were it would be a lot less dangerous than getting involved with someone as unscrupulous as Patrick Egan!'

Liz digested those revealing words in silence for a few moments. Then she said wryly, 'It seems that you know Patrick rather better than I realised. I'm sorry if I've been clumsy, but you should have warned me.'

'It's ancient history . . . ' Sarah dried her hands and walked into the living-room to sink into a chair, deciding that it was better to tell Liz a little of the truth than have her speculating and coming up with wild guesses.

Liz crossed the room to switch on the stereo. She began to sort through a pile of records, her back to Sarah. 'Feel like talking about it?' Her light tone implied an encouraging readiness to listen if she did, and a promise not to probe if she didn't. It carefully didn't convey her avid interest in finding out just what had happened to give Sarah such a dislike of a very attractive and thoroughly reliable man.

'Why not?' Sarah's voice was flat with resignation. 'It was in my first year when I really was naive and gullible. Like an idiot, I made too much of a very casual interest on his part and I've never been able to forgive him for not caring as much as I did.' It was a relief to speak openly at last of a long-hidden and long-festering hurt. 'All very youthful and very silly,' she added with sudden feeling, swamped by the realisation of the absurdity of harbouring so much hate for so long for something that she really didn't regret at all in retrospect.

For she'd gone into Patrick's arms gladly and of her own free will, and she hadn't suffered anything more than a damaged pride as a result of that brief encounter. Instead, the magic of his kiss and the ecstasy in his embrace had lived in her heart and mind ever since, and still had the power to set her body tingling with the dawn of desire. She wanted him then and she wanted him now . . . more than ever!

'Growing pains,' Liz said gently, with warm understanding. 'We all went through them, Sarah.'

'Yes, I suppose that's true.' Sarah sighed. 'But it hurt a lot and it still rankles, Liz. I'm not going to let him start where we left off just because he's come back to Hartlake.'

'I can understand that's the way you feel, of course. But if Patrick still wants you then perhaps you were more important at the time than you knew. Young doctors can't afford the time or the money or the emotion to get too involved with any girl, and if he seemed not to care or dropped you rather abruptly, it may have been a form of self-defence,' Liz pointed out shrewdly. 'It's a bit hard to penalise the poor man for something he did when you were a first-year, don't you think?'

'I'd have forgiven him more readily if he'd remembered that we knew each other when I was a first-year!'

'Oh!' Liz grimaced as she realised the full enormity of the situation. Being a woman, she could sympathise with

Sarah's humiliation at being forgotten by the one man she had remembered very well all these years. 'No wonder you're so cross with him. So should I be. But he *was* popular, you know,' she said, trying to smooth things over. 'He had an awful lot of girls swarming round him in those days . . . '

'I wasn't one of them!' Sarah exclaimed indignantly.

'No, I don't suppose you were.' Liz looked at her friend thoughtfully, remembering the shy, reserved, much too modest girl that she'd been when the rest of their set were braving Home Sister's wrath and risking life and limb by climbing through a ground-floor window of the Nurses Home to meet boyfriends and go to wild student parties when they should have been studying or sleeping in readiness for another long day on the wards. Brought up by an elderly aunt, Sarah had met few men and seemed afraid to become involved with them. She hadn't changed very much.

'I expect that's what he liked about you,' she said quietly. For everyone *had* liked the sweet-natured girl with her warm interest and readiness to help anyone in any way she could, on and off duty.

'Well, he didn't like it for long,' Sarah said dryly. 'And I expect he'd tire of me just as quickly if I relented and agreed to go out with him now. I'm not going to risk it, Liz. Let him make a fool of some other girl!'

'Harriet Blake, for instance?'

'Why not? I suppose you know that he's taking her to Founders Ball on Saturday?'

'I hope you know what you're doing, Sarah,' Liz warned lightly. 'She won't let go once she gets her clever hands on our Patrick. I know the type!'

Sarah shrugged. 'She's welcome to him!'

It wasn't true, of course. The thought of the coolly confident and rather lovely Harriet Blake in Patrick's arms, basking in the warmth of his smile and drowning in the deep waters of his ardent lovemaking twisted a knife in her breast.

'You're going with Jeff Wyman, I hear.'

'I was tempted to give it a miss this year, in fact. You know how the juniors stare and speculate about our love lives if we dance more than twice with the same man! But as everyone seems to be talking about us anyway it can only add a little fuel to the fire,' Sarah said indifferently.

'And it might blow some smoke into a certain surgeon's eyes,' Liz suggested.

'That is *not* the intention!' But Sarah had the grace to blush at the affectionate scepticism in her friend's eyes, and she smiled ruefully.

Taking pity on her, Liz put on a record and changed the subject, nobly refraining from mentioning Patrick Egan again that evening. But it was obvious that she was bursting with unasked questions and unspoken suspicions, and Sarah found herself much too tempted to talk about the man that she ought to be dimissing with angry contempt.

She didn't stay late. Her heart and mind were in confusion as she reached the foot of the narrow staircase and paused to glance at the firmly closed door of the ground-floor flat with its lighted bell-push that seemed to be inviting her touch.

She hesitated, wishing she had the courage and the confidence and the necessary humility to ring that bell and suggest that they try to talk out the pain of the past and the conflict of the present and take the first steps towards a future when they might be friends if nothing more.

She had her hand raised to the bell-push on a sudden impulse when she heard the sound of a girl's voice inside the flat, crystal clear and carrying and unmistakably familiar. In a moment, Sarah had backed away from the door and was heading for home like a bullet from a gun, a sharp pain radiating from deep in her being and threatening to engulf her . . .

* * *

From her office desk, Sarah saw him walk into the ward and the heart that had been beating much too fast for knowing that he would shortly arrive for his usual round seemed to stop at the sight of him and then lurch with sickening effect.

Very tall, very impressive and more attractive than any man had the right to be, he surveyed the ward with its gleaming orderliness and its unhurried but very busy nursing staff. Sarah bent her dark head over the mass of paperwork on her desk as that sweeping glance reached and penetrated the panoramic window of the office.

It was unprofessional, but she pretended to be unaware of his presence. *Let him wait*, she thought on a surge of renewed hurt and reached for another folder. She'd spent a restless night, thinking about him when awake and dreaming about him when she did manage to sleep — continually recalling the impulsive moment when she'd been ready to bury the hatchet and shrivelling at the thought of her embarrassment and humiliation if he'd invited her into the flat where Harriet Blake was obviously being well entertained by the surgeon she'd earmarked as a conquest when she first arrived at Hartlake.

He hadn't wasted any time in finding comfort and consolation for her rejection of him, Sarah thought bitterly, jealous and despairing and renewing her resolve to have nothing more to do with Patrick Egan. The slightest weakening on her part only threatened to plunge her into the futility of loving a man without heart or conscience all over again . . .

A few moments later, a first-year nurse put her head round the door of the office. 'Mr Egan is on the ward and sends his compliments, Sister.'

'Thank you, Nurse.' She glanced at

her watch and shuffled the papers on her desk but made no move to get up from her chair. 'What is Staff Nurse Champion doing at the moment?'

'I think she's with Mrs Spender, Sister.'

'Well, will you go and find her and ask her to leave what she's doing for the time being and accompany Mr Egan on the round, please, Nurse. Explain that I can't spare the time myself. Apologise to Mr Egan for me, too . . . '

'Yes, Sister.' The girl hurried away, eager and excited. A student nurse only just out of the Preliminary Training School seldom had an opportunity to speak to a senior surgeon, and it would be fun to enlarge on a brief exchange with the very attractive Patrick Egan when she and the rest of her set were relating news and recounting titbits of gossip at the end of the day.

Watching through the window, Sarah saw the growing impatience in Patrick's attitude as he waited, the slight hunching of those very broad shoulders, the bunching of his hands in the deep pockets of his white coat and the jut of the strong, handsome jaw. But he had a smile for the first-year as she reached him and delivered the message, a smile that obviously flustered the very young nurse and sent her back to her work with the beginnings of a blush in her pretty face. He had that effect on women, Sarah thought dryly.

His smile faded as he glanced towards the office, and Sarah sensed rather than saw the slight shrug with which he greeted her decision to remain at her desk.

There was a little delay before Helen finally arrived to join him and she visibly brightened as the ward doors opened to admit Jeff and the other members of the surgical team. Patrick had arrived early and Sarah allowed herself to wonder if he'd hoped for a private word with her before the others arrived on the ward. Well, she'd denied him the opportunity — and denied herself the pleasure of melting at the smile in his dark eyes and the seductive warmth in his black velvet voice, she thought with a little sinking of her heart as she saw the ready smile and the quick word that he had for Harriet Blake.

She marvelled at the mix of femininity and hard-headed ambition of the blonde house officer. She could almost like the girl and admire her ability if *she* didn't so obviously like and want and mean to have Patrick, come hell or high water. She didn't seem to regard the ward sister on Mallory as a rival. Sarah's cool and snubbing manner towards the surgeon was obviously convincing. She'd almost managed to convince herself that he'd meant very little in the past and meant even less these days.

As the round started and the group in their white coats of varying lengths moved along the ward to the first of Patrick's patients, Sarah settled down to her paperwork. But it was hard to concentrate on the nursing care programme that she was drawing up for the newest of her first-years. Even without looking, she knew almost every move that Patrick made, every time he turned to Harriet Blake to examine a patient or answer a question or suggest a suitable treatment.

Having seen the girl in action on several occasions, Sarah knew that she was doing all she could to impress the surgeon with her cleverness and her confidence even while using those striking eyes to excellent effect to show him that she was a very feminine woman as well as a promising member of his surgical team.

Sarah looked up some twenty minutes later as the bustle of the team's departure from the ward caught her attention. She realised abruptly that Patrick had gone without making any attempt to see or speak to her. She was avoiding him, but it hurt that he seemed to be avoiding her, too. It hurt even more to wonder if he'd abandoned his pursuit of her to concentrate on the charms of the more encouraging Harriet Blake.

'Any problems, Staff?' She emerged from the office just as Helen Champion came along the corridor, glowing and elated.

Helen paused. 'No, Sister. It was mostly routine.'

Sarah hesitated. 'There was nothing that Mr Egan wished to discuss with me this morning, apparently.'

It was carefully casual to protect her pride. But she needn't have bothered. For Helen's head and heart were much too full of Jeff Wyman, whose smile for her had seemed to hold a special significance, to notice anything unusual about the ward sister's manner or tone of voice.

'He said there was no need to disturb you as you were so very busy, Sister.'

Sarah nodded. 'Very well . . . thank you, Staff.' She felt that the words with their sceptical and slightly mocking overtones had been meant to reach her ears. She hadn't expected to fool him with a pretence of busyness, she reminded herself — merely to emphasise her indifference to him as man or surgeon.

But it wasn't indifference that jolted her heart when he walked into the side ward later that day when she was making Mrs Spender comfortable. The old lady was making good progress despite her age and frailty and she was already demanding to be returned to the main ward. She liked the hustle and the bustle and the company of other patients as well as the reassurance of seeing nurses about the ward. Like so many old people, she distrusted the buzzer that was placed close to her hand so that she could summon a nurse if needed and she was afraid that she might be forgotten by the busy staff as they went about their work. It just couldn't happen on a well-run ward, but Sarah sympathised with her anxiety and took the time to reassure her as well as attend to her physical well-being.

Patrick had seen Mrs Spender on his round that morning and been satisfied with her condition, so this was more in the nature of a social call than a professional visit. He admired the lively old lady who wouldn't allow even extensive major surgery to quell her spirit or undermine her determination to return to the tiny terraced house where she lived alone and looked after herself with the fierce independence of her kind.

It was also an excuse to see Sarah, he admitted to himself. Annoyed that she'd delegated a staff nurse to his round and surprised that she'd allowed personal animosity to affect her professional attitude, he'd walked out of Mallory without bothering to pay her the courtesy of a word or smile. Only later, when temper had cooled, did he realise that he was making matters worse.

She was stubborn and sharp-tongued and still on the defensive, but he wanted her more than any woman he'd ever known . . . and it seemed that she might be the one woman that he'd never have, he thought dryly. For her beautiful eyes were as cold and as hard as the sapphires they resembled as she glanced up from adjusting the cannula attached to the old lady's wrist and returned his greeting in brisk and impersonal manner.

Mrs Spender was drowsy from a recent injection, but she responded to the sound of Patrick's deep voice by turning her head and managing a faint smile. For while she always enjoyed the flirtatious banter of Jeff's visits to her bedside, she had a particularly soft spot for the attractive senior surgeon. Like too many women, Sarah thought, hardening her heart and her resistance to the charm of the smile that seemed to include her in its warmth.

'How are you now, my dear?' Patrick took the frail, too-thin hand in both his own and clasped it warmly. 'No pain, I hope?' He glanced at Sarah as he spoke, knowing that the indomitable old lady would never complain.

'She's just had another injection. Mr Wyman increased the dosage as she wasn't very comfortable.'

He nodded. 'There's certainly no need for her to suffer.' He bent over the bed, knowing that his patient was slightly deaf as well as drowsy. 'I'm sorry about the pain, but we're doing all we can to make it bearable.'

'Don't you worry about me, son,' the old lady said almost chirpily, making an obvious effort. 'I know all about pain. I've had plenty in me time. We're all long livers in my family and I'm good for a few years yet!'

'Yes, I'm sure you are.' It was very confident. Patrick turned to Sarah. 'I'll just have a look at the chart, please, Sister . . . '

He skimmed quickly through the detailed observations with a practised eye while she waited for comment or instruction and tried not to admire the heart-catching good looks, the glossy black curls nestling on the nape of his neck, the broad shoulders and the strongly-sculptured hands that were so skilled at healing with the knife and so expert when it came to setting a woman on fire with the merest touch.

Hastily, Sarah reined her thoughts before they tumbled any further down that dangerous path. But it wasn't so easy to control the heart that quickened or the body that throbbed with sudden excitement as their eyes met and held.

It was the briefest of contacts, but the air was suddenly electric with the kind of emotions that had no place at all on a hospital ward. Sarah thought wryly that no amount of protest or denial would succeed in convincing him of her indifference after that sudden sparking of mutual attraction . . .

11

Sister and surgeon left the small ward and strolled along the corridor, discussing Mrs Spender's present condition and his optimistic forecast of her future. She was still very ill but he saw no reason why she shouldn't make a good recovery, Patrick declared confidently.

'I'm not sure that she'll be able to go on living alone, however,' he went on. 'I'd like to see her in some kind of sheltered accommodation that enables her to keep her independence but ensures that there's always someone at hand to keep an eye on her.'

'Perhaps the Social Services can help. I'll have a word with the Welfare Liaison Officer,' Sarah suggested.

'Yes ... do that, would you? Apparently her son is willing to take her in, but she's very much against that idea. She gets on well with her daughter-in-law and she loves the grandchildren who are all very good to her. But she doesn't approve of too many generations beneath one roof.'

'I think sheltered accommodation might well be the answer. Sadly, there are so few places and so many old people in similar need,' Sarah said ruefully. 'Mrs Spender is fortunate to have a caring family. She isn't lonely or neglected or worried about money like so many of the old who come into hospital and never want to go home.'

'She has a large and supportive family,' Patrick agreed. 'Every incentive to get well and go home, in fact. She has a family wedding in the near future and she's determined to be there. If she continues to make the kind of progress that she's made in the last twenty-four hours then I haven't the slightest doubt that she'll be the liveliest member of that wedding party!'

Sarah was surprised by the intimate knowledge of the old lady's family matters and moved by the warmth and near-tenderness of his tone. 'You really care, don't you?' she said impulsively.

He smiled. 'Well, I hope so! I've expended a lot of time and effort on my patient and I don't want to see it wasted,' he said lightly, shrugging off the suggestion of sentiment.

'It's more than that!'

He shrugged. 'I like the old lady. I admire her spirit. She's proud and stubborn and very independent . . . rather like you, in fact, Sister,' he added with the glint of a smile.

Sarah was absurdly pleased that for once the words seemed like a compliment rather than a criticism. 'All the things that you really like about me,' she laughed sceptically, slightly mocking.

Patrick looked down at the pure oval face with the delicate tinge of colour in the cheeks and amusement dancing in the dark blue eyes and his heart turned over in his breast with sudden longing. 'All the things that make me go on wanting you,' he said quietly.

Her eyes widened at the unexpected words, but she hoped she knew better than to believe the warm promise of his eyes and voice. It was too quick and too smooth, she thought levelly, and his interpretation of wanting was probably very different to her own. She might ache to be in his arms, but it was becoming much more important that she should have a lasting place in Patrick Egan's heart, although she had no intention of letting him know it.

'Flattery will get you nowhere, Mr Egan,' she told him coolly and turned to stop a hurrying first-year nurse in her tracks, disliking the way that the girl had stared at them as she came along the corridor. The surgeon might find it easy to forget their surroundings — their respective positions in the hospital hierarchy and the proximity of patients and staff — but she was very conscious of the junior's curiosity. 'One moment, Nurse Palmer! Where are you going?'

'To the linen cupboard, Sister. Staff sent me for some fresh sheets for Mrs Wilmot's bed . . . ' The girl's tone was apprehensive, for she was sure that she must be doing something wrong. In her first few days on Mallory she hadn't been able to do anything right! Just her luck to start real nursing on Sister Sour's ward, she thought ruefully — and the ward sister was living up to her nick-name with a vengeance! Crossed in love, her set had decided, knowing all about the way she was clinging to Jeff Wyman when everyone knew that he was really in love with Helen Champion . . .

Sarah looked her over with disapproval. 'Change that apron and do something about that hair before you do anything else,' she said sharply, aware that the surgeon's dark eyes rested on the blonde and pretty junior with masculine appraisal and approval in their smiling depths. 'You're a disgrace to my ward, Nurse! I'm sure Sister Tutor stressed how important it is for a nurse to look clean and tidy on the ward. No patient wishes to be nursed by someone in a badly stained apron and with hair flying all over the place!'

'No, Sister . . . ' Nurse Palmer looked down at the offending apron with a guilty expression, wishing she'd found time to change it between one job and the next and smarting at the scolding in front of a senior surgeon. She put up a hand to the thick golden curls that threatened her cap and tumbled about her youthful face, escaping the dozen or so pins that she'd used earlier in vain hope of controlling the soft, silky mass. 'I'm sorry, Sister. But it's newly washed,' she ventured.

Sarah sighed. 'Well, do what you can with it! Quickly, Nurse! Don't keep Staff waiting for ever for those sheets!' She looked after the chastened junior. 'I'm afraid that hair will always be a problem,' she said, just a little envious of the glorious colour and profusion of those curls. In her experience, men really did prefer blondes — and particularly in Patrick Egan's case! It was still a source of wonder that there had been one occasion when he'd been attracted to a girl with hair as dark as his own!

'First-years always have problems of one kind or another,' Patrick drawled, dark eyes dancing. 'Things loom so large at that age.' It was a gently mocking reminder of the intensity of an eighteen-year-old, six years before.

'I have to be hard on them,' Sarah said defensively, knowing that she'd been slightly too hard on her newest junior for all the wrong reasons.

'No one's criticising you. I think you do a marvellous job,' he told her, meaning it.

'Thank you.' She looked at him doubtfully, distrusting the compliment.

Patrick glanced at his watch. 'I must get on,' he said reluctantly. 'Am I still in disgrace or will you have a drink with me tonight, Sarah? I'll be in the Kingfisher between seven and eight . . . '

He didn't wait for an answer but was gone so quickly that only his smile lingered to kindle her heart to involuntary response. Like the Cheshire Cat, she thought — and just as unpredictable, no doubt! She wouldn't meet him for a drink, of course. That would set all the tongues wagging. What had he been thinking of to suggest so public a place, haunted by so many of the staff? He'd taken Harriet Blake into the Kingfisher for a drink and now everyone was talking of a relationship between the surgeon and the blonde house officer. Another blonde, Sarah thought heavily. What chance did a mere brunette have of making any lasting impact on Patrick Egan?

She handed over the care of the ward to Audrey Crane just after seven o'clock that evening, wondering if the night staff nurse saw anything of the surgeon these days or if the affair had fizzled out. Night duty wasn't conducive to any permanent relationship between members of the hospital staff.

It was raining when Sarah emerged into the High Street with its steady stream of traffic and a flow of people making for the hospital in time for evening visiting hours. The flower stalls were doing a brisk trade and the cars and buses and taxis were constantly being held up by the traffic lights at the pedestrian crossing.

Sarah drew her cloak about her against the chill drizzle of rain and descended the stone steps, intending to make her way directly to the car park. She glanced at the popular pub on the other side of the road and came to an abrupt halt. It seemed unkind to leave Patrick waiting, not knowing if she would turn up or not. She could just put her head inside the bar to tell him that she didn't have time for a drink that evening . . .

Almost of their own volition, her feet took her to the crossing and hurried her across to the opposite pavement as the traffic obligingly came to a standstill for her and several others. She hung back slightly as she neared the pub, recognising the couple ahead of her, but they'd seen her and held the door for her to enter. She thanked them with a quick smile and moved towards the bar, looking round for Patrick. He was easily seen, his height and build and that gleaming black hair setting him head and shoulders above every other man in the place. In more ways than one, Sarah admitted, heart leaping like a wild thing in her breast as he turned, saw her, and smiled a welcome.

The lack of surprise in his dark eyes almost made her wish that she'd disappointed the too-confident, too-attractive surgeon, but the momentary chagrin was chased away as he reached for her hand and pressed it warmly.

'Good girl,' he said softly, a glow in the deep-set dark eyes that had probably been the downfall of many women.

Sarah looked at him with a hint of mockery in her smile. 'I didn't think you had much time for good girls,' she said.

Patrick laughed and turned to the hovering barman. Drinks ordered and supplied, he picked up the glasses and indicated a corner table. 'Shall we get away from the crowd . . . ?' He slid on to the cushioned seat beside her and raised his glass of ice-cold beer to her in a silent toast. Sarah's smile was slightly strained. Heaven knew what she was doing with this man when she had no good reason to warm to him and every reason to distrust the tingling excitement in her veins and the growing awareness of his very potent sexuality. His muscular thigh was pressed against her leg and his shoulder was perilously near to brushing her cheek. She knew a very foolish longing to turn to him, to press her face to the rough tweed of his jacket and murmur his name and invite the strong arms to close about her in ardent and reassuring embrace.

'I don't know what I'm doing here,' she said abruptly, almost angrily, furious with her own weakness. 'I only came in to tell you that I wouldn't be staying for a drink!'

Patrick smiled. 'I guess you're just wax in my hands.'

'Just this one drink and then I'm going home,' she warned, admitting to herself that the light words were truer than he knew. 'We're not making a night of it!'

'Whatever you say . . . ' He shrugged, concealing disappointment and dismay.

Sarah watched him trace a careful pattern in a small spillage of beer on the table. The movement of his hands unexpectedly set up an erotic image in her mind and she shivered at the thought of them moving over her body in a slow and sensuous caress, making her weak with wanting and powerless to resist the promise in his passion. Her mind and heart and body began to throb with a longing that she was still refusing to call love, insisting that it was only a very dangerous chemistry.

Sensing her inner tumult, Patrick

turned his dark head to smile at her. 'This was a mistake,' he said quietly. 'This place is much too public for us. Isn't it, Sarah?'

Her name was a soft, lingering endearment on his lips, and the look in his eyes fluttered her heart and quickened the heady intoxication in her blood. 'It's safe!' she returned promptly.

He reached to cover her slim hand with his own. 'I wish you'd trust me. I'm not going to hurt you, Sarah. You're just wasting precious time fighting me, fighting the way we feel about each other. I *know* what's going on inside you . . . some of it, anyway! I know you want me just as much as I want you. We've a lot to give each other if only you'd admit it . . . '

It was very warm, coaxing, but slightly too smooth and too sure, Sarah decided, grimly clinging to caution and common sense. She might have lost her virginity to him six years before, swayed by his smile and his persuasive charm, but she had no intention of sacrificing pride and self-respect to his fleeting desires.

'What are *you* offering? One night of so-called love — and pretend it never happened in the bright light of day?' She laughed, shook her head. 'No, thanks. You're very glib and you know how to use that charm to good effect, but only a first-year or a fool would fall for that line — and I'm neither these days!'

His expression hardened. 'Damn your stubborn pride!' he exclaimed impatiently, throwing her hand back into her lap and sitting back to glower at his half-drunk lager.

Sarah reached for her cloak and bag. 'I must be going,' she said lightly.

He rose without a word and she brushed past him, so close that he could smell the perfume of her hair and skin mingling with the slightly antiseptic aroma of the nurse who'd spent a busy day on a hospital ward. He watched her make her way through the crush of people towards the door, a frown in his dark eyes, mingled anger and dismay burning in his chest.

Suddenly he hurried after her to catch up as she thrust through the door and emerged into the damp of the evening.

'Just a minute, Sarah!' It was curt, forceful.

She paused, glancing over her shoulder at the tall, determined surgeon. 'What is it?'

In two strides, Patrick reached her side and took her arm in a grip that brooked no argument. 'Going home, are you? I'll walk with you to your car. There's something I want to ask you . . . something I need to know,' he told her abruptly.

'Oh, if you like — but I won't guarantee that you'll get any answers!' Suspecting it was just another ploy and a preliminary to further persuasion, Sarah began to walk quickly along the wet pavements. The drizzle had turned into a downpour while they were in the Kingfisher and the gloom of the evening needed the relief of the reflected street lights and the brightly-lit shop windows.

Patrick was silent as they crossed the road and turned through the hospital gates, making their way towards the staff car park. He was trying to form words and phrases that would tactfully voice the dark thoughts that had lurked at the back of his mind for some days, troubling him. He felt it was time to clear up the mystery of a past well-remembered and still resented misunderstanding. Knowing would either put an end to wanting or give him fresh hope for the future, he decided.

At last he spoke. 'You said once that I'd given you a night to remember when we first met, and you said it in such a way that I wish to God *I* could remember — perhaps I'd know what it is you have against me,' he said quietly. 'You also implied that I was drunk. So we met one night when I was too drunk to recall anything about it. Did I try something more than a pass, Sarah? Did I lose my head and try to rape you? Is that what you won't talk about and can't forgive?'

Sarah stumbled and was glad of his firm hold on her arm as shock hit her heart and drove the blood from her cheeks. It hadn't occurred to her that he could put such a construction on her angry silence about a six-year-old hurt.

'No!' she exclaimed aghast, coming to an abrupt halt beneath one of the lamps that bordered the car park. 'It wasn't like *that*!'

Patrick expelled pent-up breath in a sigh of relief, but he was quick to realise the betrayal in the way she'd spoken and the words she'd used. It was confirmation that he'd needed of an elusive memory in his blood rather than his brain where she was concerned.

'But I did make love to you that night, Sarah.' It was a statement rather than a question. 'Against your will to some extent, perhaps? A man can get carried away after a few drinks and he doesn't always want to believe that a girl means no just because she says it.' He looked down at her pale, lovely face, and its soft beauty in the lamplight caught fiercely at his heart. 'I just can't remember and you won't explain . . . '

'Because you ought to remember!' she suddenly exploded, bitterness breaking its bounds. 'I shouldn't *have* to explain what happened! Don't you think I'm entitled to any pride, damn you! I wish *I* could erase it from my life as completely as you did!'

Patrick's heart wrenched as he saw the tear that escaped, despite all her proud effort to contain it, and trickled to mingle with the raindrops that were falling on her upturned face.

'I guess I hurt you,' he said quietly, with regret, touching tender fingers to that betraying tear. 'Whatever I did . . . '

Sarah jerked her face from the caressing touch of his hand and hardened her heart to the contrition in the deep voice. 'I was eighteen,' she said stonily. 'What was it you said earlier today . . . that things loom large at that age? Well, you loomed very large in my life that night and I thought you felt the same way about me. I was wrong.' She broke off, swallowing the bitterness of remembered rejection and humiliation.

'Oh, Sarah,' he said achingly, with love, suddenly sure that she was the one woman he wanted by his side for the rest of his life. He slid his arms beneath the folds of her warm cloak and drew her into him — lowered his head to kiss her with infinite tenderness that was a plea for forgiveness and a new beginning.

Sarah's lips quivered. For a moment, pain and pride were both forgotten as reluctant but insistent love and longing swelled her heart and desire leaped like a flame to meet the heavy throb of passion in the lean, hard body so close to her own.

For a moment, they stood together in the shadow of Hartlake, sister and surgeon, knowing the mutual if unspoken need to touch, to kiss, to feel the nearness of each other. Rain fell steadily, unnoticed.

There was more than the passion of a man for a woman in the way that Patrick held her, enfolding her in a love that would last for a lifetime. The incredible sweetness of her lips and the yielding softness of her slender body filled him with a new and joyous confidence in a future they would surely share.

Sarah clung to the delight in that kiss, but she was still reluctant to trust him, to surrender the pride that had protected her all these years from being hurt again by any man. She desperately needed to be loved and she couldn't believe that there was anything more than a familiar urgency of desire in the way that Patrick had caught her close and taken possession of her lips.

He raised his head but continued to hold her against his heart. 'This is how it's meant to be for us,' he told her firmly. 'Don't run away from me any more, Sarah. It's such a waste of our lives to fight what we have going for each other. I want you so much and I know I can make you happy . . . ' He'd never asked any woman to marry him. He hadn't known that the right words would be so elusive when it was so important to find them.

Sarah drew away, pain like a knife in her breast. She wanted him, too. But not in the way that he was suggesting. Not to know a too brief ecstasy in his arms and then the terrible emptiness of life without him when he tired of her, as he inevitably would.

'No,' she said flatly.

'Please, Sarah.' He'd never pleaded for any woman in his life. It had never been necessary. But now he would beg her on his knees to marry him if that was the only way to convince her that she was the only woman he wanted, now and forever.

She shook her head. 'You're not getting the chance to hurt me again,' she told him with cold finality, denying the cry of her heart to be allowed its own chance of happiness or despair.

'Oh, *darling* . . . !' Patrick moved to take her back into his arms, desperate to convince her of his integrity and his sincerity and hoping to persuade her in the intimacy of his embrace, but she backed from him and there was such a blaze in her beautiful eyes that he was checked in the impulsive movement.

'Don't call me that! And don't dare to touch me or kiss me again — ever! You don't seem to understand just how much I hate you!'

Sarah almost choked on her fury as she threw the words at him. For hadn't he called her 'darling' in just that soft and tender and utterly meaningless fashion on that memorable night when she'd pleased and delighted this sensual man with her eager response to his ardent lovemaking? He'd held her and kissed her and called her 'darling' as though she would be eternally dear, and she'd foolishly believed it and clung to him and allowed him to sweep her with him to the towering peaks of an undreamed-of ecstasy. He'd murmured *darling* once more against her lips in the tumultuous finale of passion — and at their very next meeting he'd looked through her as if they were complete strangers!

She'd smiled at him shyly and with the dawn of love — and received in return a blank, preoccupied stare that left her in no doubt at all that it wasn't discretion or lack of recognition, but lack of all interest. Sarah had discovered in that painful moment the truth of the adage that a man never values what is too easily attained.

How could he now expect to be forgiven, to be taken into her arms as a lover all over again? It was six years too late for Patrick Egan to decide that he wanted her still.

Before a dismayed Patrick could say or do anything to combat that furious veto on a future he wished to spend with her, Sarah had fled, running in the rain, cloak flying.

There was no point in following, he realised, heavy at heart. She'd made it very clear how she felt about him and how hopeless it was for him to love the proud and stubborn and spirited Sister Sweet . . .

12

Tired and tense and troubled, Sarah stood at the window of her sitting-room just along the corridor from the ward and rested her hot and aching head against the pane while her forgotten tea cooled in its cup. She had been glad to escape for a while from the demands of her work and the proximity of patients and staff. For even the job that she dearly loved wasn't able to dispel the constant ache somewhere in the region of her heart.

She looked down at the sunny square of garden set between the tall hospital buildings and graced by the central statue of the hospital's founder, Sir Henry Hartlake. From that height, it wasn't possible to make out the faces of the people who hurried along the criss-crossing paths *en route* to various departments, but doctors and students, nurses, physiotherapists and lab technicians, hospital porters and other ancillary staff were all easily identified by their varying and distinctive uniforms.

Even knowing that Patrick was busy in Theatres, Sarah was still consciously searching for him among the men who walked briskly through the garden, long white coats flapping in the breeze. She knew that he would be quite easily recognisable with his height and those broad shoulders and the authority in his stride.

The need to see him was beginning to dominate her every thought, waking and sleeping. She hadn't seen or spoken to him since she'd run from him in the rain. The following day she'd been off duty and thankful not to be working on the busy surgical ward with its many demands after a night when she had tossed and turned in restless regret and longing.

This morning she'd braced herself for the inevitable meeting, but Jeff had arrived to take the round with the explanation that his boss was dealing with an emergency in Theatres.

Patrick's failure to get in touch with her spoke volumes, Sarah felt. She'd dealt him the final rebuff and she couldn't expect him to swallow his considerable pride for her sake.

She sighed.

A knot of nurses were relaxing on the lawn below in a flurry of blue check frocks, released from lectures to sit in the sunshine with their textbooks during the morning break, first-years who had not yet graduated to the wards from the Preliminary Training School and were always referred to indulgently by senior staff as Pets.

It seemed a very long time to Sarah since she'd been one of a similar group, impatient with the schoolroom and theory and long lists of bones and muscles,lifesize dummy patients and hours of practise with bedpans and bandages, eager to get on with the business of nursing real people in real situations on the wards. Life in those first weeks at Hartlake had been all study and confusion and doubt that she'd ever make state registration, but at least it hadn't been complicated by Patrick Egan.

That had happened some months later, towards the end of her first year, with exams looming. She was working on Paterson and he was a houseman on a surgical team. All the juniors apparently admired and sighed over him and one or two of them managed to interest him for a short time. With his dark good looks and casual charm, he was very attractive and took advantage of his many opportunities for flirtation and sexual conquest, like most of his colleagues.

Sarah was shy and innocent and hard-working, and unlike most of her set she seldom took any part in the social whirl. Patrick Egan never appeared to notice her, on or off the ward. So she was totally unprepared for his flattering admiration and pursuit at that fateful party. Being very young and inexperienced, her head and heart filled with romantic dreams of love and happy-ever-after, she'd been swept off her feet by his ardent persuasions and her own suddenly-awakened sexuality.

That was forgivable at eighteen. But it was the height of folly for a mature and sensible ward sister to come so close to surrendering a second time to that devastating, dangerous charm, the enchantment in the deep velvet voice and the promise of heaven here and now in those smiling dark eyes.

Foolish but terribly, terribly tempting . . .

She turned as the door opened on a light tap. 'Yes, Staff . . . what is it?' There was the slightest of snaps in her tone, for she relied on her senior staff nurse to carry on in her temporary absence from the ward and she felt she was entitled to fifteen minutes' break in a busy morning.

'It's time for Mrs Spender's pethidine, Sister.' Helen was surprised that the usually ultra-efficient Sarah Sweet needed the reminder, and it certainly wasn't like her to be off the ward for so long without warning.

'Not yet, surely!' Frowning, Sarah checked her watch and was shocked to discover that she'd been dreaming about Patrick for almost forty minutes. 'Well, what's the problem, Staff?' she demanded, cross with herself and venting some of that irritation on the unoffending staff nurse. 'Can't you cope with a straightforward injection?'

'Yes, of course, Sister. If I may have the key to the drug cupboard . . . ?'

Sarah bit her lip at the demure reply that nevertheless held reproach. 'Oh . . . I'm sorry! I thought I'd left the keys with you. I've rather a lot on my mind this morning, I'm afraid . . . ' She unclipped the bunch of keys from her belt and gave them to Helen with a rueful smile.

Helen looked at her curiously. 'Are you well, Sister? You're looking pale. Can I get you some aspirin?'

'Thank you, but I'm perfectly well, Staff. Just a little tired after a late night.' It was said as brightly as if she'd spent the evening in revelry instead of alone and fretting over the regretted rejection of a man she finally admitted to wanting with all her heart.

She'd gone to bed early but it had been almost impossible to sleep with Patrick's image so vividly etched on her closed eyelids, every word they'd recently exchanged echoing in her thoughts and her body restless and yearning for the man who had the power to fire her to desire at a touch.

If it wasn't love that had possession of her heart and mind and body and threatened to turn her whole world upside down, then it was something too like it for comfort, she thought wryly.

As the staff nurse left the room, Sarah grimaced at the cup of cold tea on the tray. She really must pull herself together. A ward sister with the weight of so much responsibility on her shoulders just couldn't afford to spend half the morning in a fantasy world where she was loved and needed by the only man who had ever meant anything, she told herself firmly.

Helen almost collided with Jeff Wyman in the corridor. He winked at her, 'Sister about?'

Helen indicated the sitting-room. 'In there.'

Jeff nodded. 'Thanks.' He paused. 'How are you this morning, sweetheart?'

'Rushed off my feet.' But she hesitated and smiled. 'Is there anything I can do? Sister isn't feeling too good.'

'You can do a lot for me, Helen,' he told her lightly, sliding an arm about her waist and stealing a quick kiss in the temporarily empty corridor. '*Later* . . . '

Helen watched as he knocked lightly and admitted himself to the sitting-room with the air of being sure of a warm and possibly even intimate welcome. She went on to the clinical room to collect the pethidine for Mrs Spender's injection, tormenting herself with all kinds of images of what might be going on behind that closed door. She was desperately jealous of his friendship with Sarah Sweet, although it didn't keep him from stringing *her* along with compliments and promises and the occasional date. It wasn't enough for Helen, and she felt that if Sarah Sweet wasn't around there might be a better chance of finding a lasting happiness with the good-looking Jeff Wyman. But she *was* around, and there didn't seem any likelihood that she would leave Hartlake in the near future.

Unless she had reason to do so . . .

Jeff closed the door behind him, smiling at Sarah.

'That isn't wise,' she said dryly. 'All the juniors will be speculating wildly.'

'Let them.' He put his arms about her, smiling into her eyes with a hint of mischief in his own. 'If they say that

269

I'm making love to you, they'll be right, won't they?'

'No.' Sarah drew away, rigid with rejection.

'Something wrong?' he asked quietly. 'Helen said you aren't feeling well.'

'I'm fine.' She was instantly annoyed that he'd been discussing her with the staff nurse.

'Is there any tea in that pot?' He sat down as if he intended to make a long stay.

'It's cold, I'm afraid. I can order some fresh . . . ' But she glanced at her watch rather pointedly and her tone didn't invite acceptance.

'No, don't bother, love. I need a break more than tea, quite honestly. It's been hectic without Patrick this morning. He's dealing with a nasty case . . . a lad with multiple injuries after smashing his father's car. I don't rate his chances too highly, even with Patrick pulling out all the stops.'

'You like him, don't you?' Sarah felt the sudden need to have her own growing admiration and respect for the surgeon supported by the spoken approval of a colleague.

Jeff hesitated. 'Well, we aren't exactly bosom friends,' he said carefully. 'We get on and I'm learning a lot from him, but I don't think he has too much time for me, to be frank.' He didn't add that there was rivalry between them that had more to do with Sarah than their respective jobs. Egan played his cards very close to his chest, but Jeff suspected his interest in Sarah and he wasn't deceived by her pretence of indifference towards the man. They'd known each other too long and that icy manner was slightly overdone, he felt. Like too many women, if Egan made a serious play for her she'd probably fall into his hands like a ripe plum . . . 'All set for tomorrow night, Sarah?'

'Yes, I think so . . . ' She tried to sound enthusiastic but she felt even less like going to Founders Ball with him. She kept remembering that Patrick had wanted to take her and she'd refused him . . .

She managed to hustle Jeff out of her sitting-room and took him along the corridor to the ward office, much less private and less prone to exciting speculation among the juniors. Helen was standing at the drugs trolley, checking the level of a hypodermic syringe. The trolley was always kept locked and in a prominent position in the corridor just outside the office, chained to a ring in the wall when not in use for security reasons.

As though her return was the signal for everything to erupt, Sarah scarcely had time to breathe for the next half-hour. The telephone never stopped ringing. Nurses besieged her with urgent queries and requests. An irate husband, tired of waiting for attention, stormed the office in a belligerent mood and had to be soothed and his questions duly answered. A first-year fainted and had to be revived with sal volatile and then packed off to sick bay, and a quarrel that could be heard at the far end of the ward broke out between two ward-maids in the kitchen. Thankful that Jeff had gone away some time before, Sarah flew to silence the fracas with a few well-chosen words. Sister Sour with a vengeance!

Then it was time for the midday medicine round and Sarah went to unchain the trolley and check its contents, diving her hand into her pocket for the keys. Her hand came out empty. The keys weren't clipped to her belt as they ought to be. Frowning, she went in search of Helen Champion and found her in the sluice.

'I think you still have the keys, Staff,' she said, rather crossly.

Helen shook her head. 'No, Sister.'

Sarah's mouth tightened. 'What do you mean? You must have them! You came to me for them when it was time for Mrs Spender's injection.'

'I brought them back to you,' Helen said firmly.

Sarah's brows snapped together.

Mislaying the ward keys was tantamount to losing the Crown Jewels — if not worse! 'When did you bring them back?'

'When you were dealing with Mr Ellis, Sister. You took them from me and put them down on the desk.'

'I did *what*!' Sarah was horrified. It was a primary rule that the keys were always passed from hand to hand and never laid down anywhere, for a busy or briefly distracted nurse could forget to pick them up again. Dangerous drugs had to be locked away securely and it was the responsibility of the senior nurse in charge to know where the keys to the trolley and drugs cupboard were at all times.

She almost ran to the office with Helen on her heels and swept files and forms from the cluttered desk in a futile hunt for the keys. The two nurses looked at each other with foreboding and began a frantic search of the room while Sarah thought with dread of what she would say to Matron and the hospital committee. She would be severely reprimanded for negligence at the very least, she thought heavily.

It was Helen who found the missing keys in the waste basket where they might just have been knocked from the desk by a careless hand.

Sarah felt sick, far from relieved. She had been rushed off her feet and there had been a great deal of unusual commotion; she knew that her mind hadn't been entirely on her work that morning. Had she really left the keys on the desk and then left the office empty while she persuaded Mr Ellis to return to the waiting-room to wait for his wife to come back from the X-ray department? She couldn't even remember seeing or speaking to Helen, let alone taking the keys from her hand!

Several people had been in and out of the office during the relevant period and there had been so much confusion that it would have been easy for anyone to pick up the keys, so opportunely left on the desk, and then return later when the office was empty to drop them into the waste basket where they might seemingly have fallen by accident.

'You'd better come with me, Staff. I must check the drug cupboard right away,' Sarah said quietly, a cold hand closing about her heart, for it was a situation that everyone who held a position of authority in a hospital always dreaded.

'You surely don't think . . . '

'I hope I'm wrong!' Sarah headed for the door. She felt it was unlikely that anyone would approach the trolley, standing in full view of the office in a busy corridor. But the dangerous drugs were kept in a cabinet in the clinical room, to be issued by herself or the nurse in charge when required, and there might have been an opportunity for someone to steal what they wanted when everyone else was busy about the ward.

The two nurses checked the stock against the carefully-kept book. A small phial of amphetamine tablets was soon found to be missing.

Sarah closed and locked the cupboard door with automatic efficiency, knowing it was much too late to be so careful. She turned to Helen. 'I'm sorry, but I have to ask you, Staff,' she said formally. 'Do you know anything at all about these missing drugs?'

'No, Sister.'

Sarah nodded, accepting the denial. She had no reason to doubt the word of a girl who had always been a reliable, responsible and trustworthy nurse.

'You were the last person to handle the keys, to the best of my knowledge,' she said carefully. 'I shall have to say that I can't remember their return, which means that you'll be asked that question by a number of people. I've no doubt that you *did* bring them back, of course.'

She saw that the girl's hands were trembling as she held the stock book and she smiled at her reassuringly, although she felt ill and trembly herself at the thought of all she would have to face in the coming weeks. 'You've nothing to worry about, Helen. Matron might comment that you should have made sure that I'd clipped the keys to my belt, but you were rushed, too. No blame can attach to you on that score. I'm entirely to blame for what happened.'

'Does it mean you'll lose your job?' It was abrupt, anxious.

Sarah stared at her. 'Well, obviously. You aren't a first-year, Helen. You know as well as I do that it's a very serious offence for a sister to allow her ward keys to go missing. And as some dangerous drugs have been stolen as a result of my negligence, I shall be suspended from duty and have to appear before a disciplinary board. Of course I shall lose my job! I may never be allowed to nurse again!'

Helen bit her lip. 'I suppose that's true . . .'

Sarah turned to the door, bracing herself for action. 'I must ask every nurse if they've handled the keys or been to this cupboard or seen anyone else do so. Then I'd better report the matter to Matron,' she said briskly.

'Just a minute . . . !'

She turned, slightly impatient. There was a difficult time ahead of her and, being Sarah, she wanted to get it over as soon as possible. 'What is it, Staff?'

Helen hesitated briefly. Then she held out her hand, open to reveal the missing phial with its full complement of tablets. 'Here's the amphetamines.'

Sarah was too flooded with relief to wonder in that first instant at the miraculous reappearance of the missing drugs. 'You've found them! Thank heavens! Where on earth were they hiding?' she demanded thankfully.

'In my pocket.' It had seemed so easy and it had been the impulse of a moment, born of resentment and jealousy. But Helen had suddenly discovered that she couldn't go through with the charade, after all. She wasn't prepared to have Sarah Sweet's certain disgrace and probable dismissal on her conscience for the rest of her life.

Sarah closed the door. 'You do know what you're saying?' she asked quietly, dismay and disappointment stirring as she saw defiant challenge in the staff nurse's eyes. A defiance born of guilt and shame, she realised bleakly.

Helen nodded. 'I took the damn things.'

'But *why*? Why would you do such a silly thing? You don't take drugs, do you?'

'No.'

Sarah searched her face. 'Did you steal them for someone else?' she asked quietly.

The staff nurse winced as the word with all its ugly implications struck home. 'I didn't actually steal them,' she defended herself swiftly. 'I was going to put them back after a few hours.'

'But . . . why take them at all?' Sarah was bewildered.

280

'To get you into trouble, I suppose,' Helen admitted.

'I see . . . ' But Sarah *didn't* see and she was hurt, for she'd always thought that they were pretty good friends and it was a blow to discover herself so disliked by a fellow nurse. 'You must have a reason,' she said slowly.

Helen shrugged. 'No reason.' It was stony.

'Oh, come on!' Sarah said quickly. 'I've obviously said or done something that you didn't like and you wanted to pay me back for it! This isn't like you at all, Helen.' She remembered that the girl hadn't been the same since Jeff had come to work at Hartlake and a suspicion crystallised. 'Look, I don't want to pry but you've made it my business with this silliness,' she went on firmly. 'Is this something to do with Jeff Wyman? I know you like him. Do you think I'm standing in your way?'

'Aren't you?' Helen demanded bitterly. 'He just doesn't see me when you're around — and you don't even care about him! You're just using him!'

'Using him?' Sarah frowned. 'I don't know what you mean.'

'I've seen the way you look at Patrick Egan when he isn't looking at you! You've been panting after him for weeks — and parading Jeff like a bloody banner in case he realises it! It's so dishonest!'

Sarah disliked the coarse description of the ache of longing that Patrick evoked and she hated the thought that it was obvious to one person, at least.

She looked at Helen thoughtfully. 'You're in no position to accuse anyone of dishonesty,' she said dryly, bringing the blood rushing to the staff nurse's cheeks. But, knowing how much it hurt to feel unloved, unwanted, she was suddenly sorry for the girl. She turned to unlock the drugs cabinet and restore the phial of amphetamines to its rightful place.

'I think we should both forget all that's been said in this room,' she decided generously, feeling that the caring and conscientious nurse would be punished enough by her own remorse. 'Fortunately no real harm was done and I don't intend to report the matter to Matron or mention it to anyone. You and I were the only ones who knew that the keys were missing — oh, but they weren't really missing at all, I suppose! You very conveniently *found* them . . . where you'd dropped them, no doubt!' She sighed. 'It was easy to make a fool of me, wasn't it, Helen?'

'I'm sorry.' Helen looked and obviously felt discomfited. 'Suddenly everything was happening at once on the ward and it just seemed an opportunity to make things unpleasant for you so that you'd have to leave Hartlake. It was horrid and stupid and I don't deserve to get away with it. So if you *want* to report me to Matron . . . '

Sarah shook her head. 'I don't think it would serve any purpose. You're a good nurse and we all do silly things at times. I'm glad you had enough sense to produce the tablets and admit to taking them before anyone else knew that they were missing. Just give me your word that you'll never do anything like it again and we'll forget about it . . .'

Overwrought, utterly contrite and ashamed of herself, the staff nurse dropped her face into her hands and began to cry. Wisely, Sarah allowed her to weep for a few moments and then briskly bade her pull herself together, go and wash her face and then join her to assist with the delayed medicine round. The sharp tone was effective.

Sarah looked after the departing girl and hoped that she'd done the right thing. She had forgiven and promised to forget a momentary aberration, but it might be symptomatic of an instability of character that she hadn't suspected. She decided to keep a watchful eye on her senior staff nurse for the next few weeks. Being in love just wasn't a good enough excuse for such irresponsible behaviour in a trained nurse, after all.

It didn't excuse her own inattention to the responsibilities of her job, either, she told herself crossly. She ought to have known much sooner that the keys were not on her belt and, knowing the rigid insistence on rules drummed into her since she first came to Hartlake, she certainly ought to have doubted the nurse's claim that she'd laid them down on the desk when they'd been returned to her.

Sarah reminded herself firmly that while she might very well be in love, she was first and foremost a Hartlake nurse . . .

13

Sitting with Jeff and some friends at a cluster of tables on the edge of the dance floor, Sarah listened with only half an ear to the flow of conversation and the music that filled the crowded ballroom in the administration wing. Her dark blue eyes were intent on scanning the dancing couples for another sight of Patrick and his partner.

She'd just caught a glimpse of him, tall and dark and heart-stoppingly handsome in a fashionable grey velvet cord suit, whirling Harriet Blake around as though he didn't have a care in the world. As if he hadn't given *her* a second thought since that encounter in the car park, Sarah decided with a painful throb of her heart.

She'd relieved those moments so many times, his words echoing again and again in her mind and heart. For supposing he had really meant them? Supposing he had changed as he'd claimed, and he'd been offering her much more than she'd realised in the blazing heat of a fury born of fear. Supposing he loved her!

Sarah's heart tilted and shook at that daring and unlikely hope. She wished she hadn't flown at him so furiously that night. She wished that she'd stayed in his arms and allowed the years to sweep back so that she could remember what it had been like to tremble on the verge of loving him.

Angry and afraid, she'd said things that she didn't mean and had instantly regretted. For the way she felt about Patrick had nothing to do with *hate*.

She loved him — and she didn't want to be locked out of his arms and his life any longer by her bitter and obstinate refusal to forgive and forget. He'd called her sour and stubborn — and so she had been all these weeks, she admitted ruefully. She'd been resentful that chance had brought him back to Hartlake to revive all the memories of hurt and humiliation that she'd suffered because he hadn't valued the precious gift of herself, six year ago.

Her heart had been ready to love all over again. But pride had stood in the way. Now, if she didn't sweeten and soften and admit to wanting him, she was going to lose him to someone like the blonde and beautiful and very determined Harriet Blake, Sarah thought heavily as her searching gaze found the warm honey colour of the stylish frock that the young doctor was wearing.

The ash-blonde hair framed her face and, without the horn-rimmed glasses, she looked very young and very feminine — vulnerable. Patrick had a seemingly protective arm about her as they danced and a smile in his eyes as he looked down at the girl, apparently oblivious to everyone and everything else.

Sarah was abruptly consumed with a jealousy so fierce and so frightening that she was appalled. Did she really want to tear that lovely frock from the girl's back and cut it into shreds with her sharpest pair of surgical scissors? Did she really want to pull out handfuls of that shining hair and scratch the smile from that confident face with her bare hands? Did she really want to thrust her out of Patrick's arms and shout at the top of her voice that he belonged to *her* and no one else?

It might not be civilised behaviour or approved conduct for a Hartlake sister, but it would give her a great deal of satisfaction, she admitted with wry honesty.

Sarah was shaken to realise just how much he meant to her and how much it mattered that he should care for her, need her, want her in his life. He was her love, her destiny, her past and present and future — and she'd rejected him so furiously and with such scorn that she was sick with the fear that she might never have another chance to know the enchantment of his embrace and the promise of his pursuit. For Patrick was proud as well as passionate, and he didn't need to bother with a woman who didn't seem to want him when there were so many Harriet Blakes ready to hold out eager and welcoming arms.

Sarah was proud, too. It had been pride that kept her from greeting him with a light-hearted reminder of the previous night's encounter that he seemed to have forgotten in the rush of an overworked young houseman's busy morning, six years before. It had been pride, the fear of being suspected of running after him, that had kept her out of his way in the few weeks that remained of his compulsory year of 'walking the wards' at Hartlake, before he left to take up an appointment at another hospital to work for his FRCS.

And that same stubborn pride had kept her out his arms ever since he'd returned to Hartlake. For he'd trampled on her hopeful heart and delicate dreams, and she hadn't been able to trust him not to do it again.

She still didn't trust him. But, suddenly, nothing mattered but the need for even short-lived happiness in the arms of a man that she'd never really ceased to love, all the long and lonely years.

Jeff touched her arm lightly, rousing her from reverie. 'Sorry, love — I'm neglecting you!' he declared penitently. 'Do you want to dance? Shall we show this crowd how the experts do it?'

Sarah didn't feel like dancing. Not with Jeff, much as she liked him, grateful though she was for his affection, the support of his friendship and the welcome camouflage of caring for him that protected her heart and her vulnerable pride from the perception of her friends and colleagues.

But she found a smile for him, got to her feet and let him lead her out to the floor, tall and slim and lovelier than she knew in the soft yellow silk frock, a matching ribbon twined through the gleaming knot of dark curls worn high on her head.

Jeff's style of dancing was as extrovert as everything else about him, and Sarah was conscious of amused murmurs and indulgent smiles as he swept her around the floor to the music. He was full of light-hearted and inconsequential chatter that scarcely allowed her to concentrate on her steps as they danced. She did her best to keep up with his extravagant skips and swirls and tried not to show how much she disliked the flamboyance that drew so much attention.

He whirled her to a halt as the music stopped, looking so pleased with his own expertise that it was impossible for Sarah not to laugh . . . and, laughing at him with tender and indulgent affection, she looked over his shoulder and directly into Patrick's smouldering eyes.

Her heart missed a beat.

With his arm still about Harriet, he swept her away without so much as a smile or a word for his assistant registrar or the ward sister whose eyes had met his own for that brief moment.

Sarah's heart plummeted.

Jeff looked after the couple, shaking his head. 'Didn't even see us!' he declared. 'It must be love!' He drew Sarah's hand through his arm as he took her back to their table. 'It looks like a match, doesn't it?'

Sarah's heart felt gripped by a vice as pain and panic suddenly shot through her breast. 'Do you think so?' she asked, carefully light, carefully indifferent, feeling that she was expected to make some comment. For weren't the affairs of their colleagues of primary importance to almost everyone at Hartlake? Jimmy, the head porter, had always known and traded on that interest with his love of romance and inclination for gossip. Jeff's words made her wonder if everyone but herself knew that Patrick's interest in the blonde house officer was likely to lead to marriage. 'He isn't the type to settle down with one woman.' The rider was for her own comfort rather than merely to challenge Jeff's verdict.

He shrugged. 'You know the man better than I do, of course. But he's reached the age and the point in his career when it might be expedient for him to have a wife. He's close to a consultancy and hospital boards like their consultants to be married, you know. It presents a picture of stability, apparently. I shall have to resign myself to the same fate one of these days,' he added, grinning. 'Going to wait for me, Sarah?'

She smiled at him, sitting down. 'I've no plans to marry anyone else at the moment,' she returned brightly. She didn't think he was serious. But she was terribly afraid that Patrick might be seriously in search of a wife and, having failed in his pursuit of herself, had turned to the much more encouraging and eminently suitable Harriet Blake.

'Does that mean we're engaged?' Jeff's grey eyes twinkled at her as he sat down, tucking his long legs beneath the table and reaching for his drink.

'You'd hate it if I said yes!' Sarah regarded him with affectionate amusement. 'That tongue will get you into trouble one of these days! You'll say that kind of thing to some girl who thinks you mean it, and you won't be able to wriggle out of walking down the aisle by her side!'

Jeff didn't smile. He looked at her thoughtfully. 'Doesn't it occur to you that I mean every word and that I might want to walk down the aisle with you?'

'Please don't,' she said quickly, taking fright at the unexpected gravity of his tone and his expression. 'Let's keep things just the way they are, Jeff!'

'Nothing stands still, Sarah,' he said quietly. 'We've come to the crossroads, love. I've been patient but now you must make up your mind whether we go on together — and I do mean *together* — or go our separate ways.'

'Can't we go on being friends?'

He shook his head. 'It just isn't enough any more,' he told her bluntly.

Sarah bit her lip. She'd known that she would have to face this problem sooner or later. He had been patient and she'd given him very little in return for a wealth of liking and attention. It wasn't possible for her to give anything more, but she didn't want to lose his affection and his friendship. She was torn.

'You don't really want to marry me,' she said lamely.

'No,' he agreed. 'Not at the moment, anyway. But if things went well . . . with us, with my job . . . ' He shrugged. 'Who knows . . . ?'

It was typically light, typically Jeff. But Sarah wondered if she'd been blind and insensitive to a growing involvement on his part. It seemed unlikely, but had he been falling in love while she was merely grateful for the comfort and security of his friendship?

She hoped not, but she was puzzled by the suddenly serious overture for a man who'd always seemed even less likely than Patrick to want a permanent and meaningful relationship with anyone.

She couldn't agree, of course. She couldn't even consider his suggestion. He was a dear — warm-hearted and generous and kind, and she was very fond of him — but she could never marry him! She would probably never marry, she thought heavily. She would just carry on nursing, growing older and more suited to her nickname and eventually becoming a figure of fun to the juniors with the passing years. Sarah shrivelled at the bleak thought — and found herself wondering if it would be so impossible to stifle the need for one man in the arms of another. There was obviously no future in loving Patrick. There might be a future for her with someone like Jeff . . . one day.

'What are you suggesting? Some kind of trial run?' she asked carefully.

'If that's what you want to call it. Come and live with me and we'll see how it goes. Or we call it a day and stop seeing each other.' It was an unmistakable ultimatum.

Sarah wondered why he had chosen to confront her with such a decision on the night of Founders Ball. Despite that momentary depression and the thoughts it had prompted, there was only one answer she could give. But it seemed a pity to spoil the evening or embarrass either of them before their friends.

'Well, I don't have to say yes or no at this moment, do I?' she said lightly.

Jeff smiled. 'That's my answer, isn't it?'

She tried to explain, to soften the blow. 'We haven't known each other very long, Jeff . . . only a few weeks. I don't want to rush into anything . . . '

He looked away, a nerve throbbing in his lean cheek. 'It's Egan, isn't it?

I've pretended not to know how you feel about him, but it's always been Egan, I think. *I* know he isn't interested and *you* know he isn't interested, but you're so obsessed with him that you don't really see me or any other man.' It was rueful rather than angry. 'Well, I just can't compete with him any longer, Sarah. Frankly, I don't think there's any point in trying. I'm sorry.'

'I'm sorry, too.' Sarah didn't attempt to deny the truth of his accusation. She knew he wouldn't believe her. She was dismayed by her transparency, terrified that Patrick as well as Helen Champion and Jeff had seen through that poor pretence of indifference.

Jeff rose and walked over to where Helen was sitting with some friends, a short distance away. Sarah saw the girl's face light up as he asked her to dance and the eagerness with which she went into his arms after one quick, doubtful glance in Sarah's direction.

She was saddened that Jeff had apparently come close to loving her instead of the staff nurse who had never made much secret of the way she felt about him. But loving wasn't a matter of choice, she reminded herself. Life would be a lot less complicated if it was!

As the table emptied, friends getting up to dance, Sarah was left alone to watch the swirl of light and colour and movement and to observe the sudden radiance in Helen's pretty face as Jeff exerted his considerable and very effective charm.

Consciously looking for Patrick with a dull ache in her breast, she wondered if there was any way that she could approach the surgeon, any way that she would ever find happiness with him after all she'd said and done in the past weeks. She turned, startled, at a touch on her shoulder and the sound of his deep voice.

'I promised to dance with you, Sister — and I hope I'm a man of my word.'

Sarah stiffened. For he didn't have

to take pity on her because she was sitting alone . . . a wallflower instead of the belle of the ball! Proud, starch from head to toe, she looked up at him with a cool little smile. 'Thank you . . . but I'm sitting this one out, Mr Egan.'

Patrick frowned. 'Do you want me to drag you out by your hair?' he demanded, impatient with the antagonism that had its roots in the past and no place in the present. He reached for her hands and drew her to her feet, none too gently.

Sarah flushed with annoyance but, aware of watching and curious eyes and knowing that the grapevine would seize with eager delight on even the hint of a clash between a sister and a surgeon, she allowed him to lead her to the edge of the dance floor.

As Patrick put an arm about her, there was proud resistance in every line of her slender body and militancy in the sparkling sapphire eyes. 'This is the promised highlight of my evening,

I suppose,' she said in scathing and sardonic tones.

'I don't care what you call it. Just shut up and dance.' It was brusque enough to shock and her eyes widened. Then his arms tightened and he pulled her close and urged her into movement with the pressure of his powerful body.

The music was slow, sensuous, unexpectedly romantic, and the floor was crowded with couples taking advantage of the mood. Sarah was only aware of Patrick, his nearness and his dearness, as her treacherous body began to throb and her pulses quickened to the heavy thud of his heart against her soft breast.

The stiffness seeped out of her and she pressed close to him, fingers straying from his shoulder to twine in the glossy black curls on the nape of his neck that were an irresistible invitation to any woman's touch. She felt the brush of his lips across her hair, her brow, the curve of her cheek, and her heart faltered and then leaped with new hope. For he was making unmistakable love to her with those light kisses, the sensual pressure of his lean, hard body, the slow stroke of his strong hands across her back and shoulders.

She couldn't doubt the degree of his wanting. Or her own, Sarah admitted, consumed by the tumultuous, tormented flame. Perhaps it was madness to betray it as she so obviously did in the way she melted against him and turned her face slightly as his lips hovered like a question mark at the corner of her mouth. It was the merest of butterfly kisses as their lips touched, but it was admission and surrender on her part. Sarah no longer cared. Nothing mattered any more but the love and the need and the knowledge that he was her destiny, come what may.

The tension ebbed out of him on a sigh of satisfaction. The music continued to flow about them but he stopped, holding her against him, a glow in his dark eyes that set her trembling and turned her into a weak and helpless wanton all over again, eager for his loving even if she might never know his love.

'Tell Wyman that you're leaving with me,' he commanded. 'If he can't look after you better then he deserves to lose you. You know my car, Sarah! It'll be outside the door in five minutes . . .'

Releasing her abruptly, he strode towards the nearest exit with a purposeful air that parted the crowd for him. Sarah looked after him, knowing that she should be annoyed by that abrupt desertion and the arrogant assumption that she would do his bidding. But the tattoo of her heart, the molten fire in her veins and the whirling intoxication at the thought of his embrace, the ecstasy that she'd craved for so long, left no room for anything so mundane and unimportant as anger or pride.

Patrick was waiting in the car. As she emerged from the building, he leaned to open the passenger door, relief glimmering in the dark eyes, for he hadn't been as confident of the outcome as he'd appeared, knowing her proud and bitter obstinacy of past weeks. Sarah hesitated and then slid into the seat beside him with a pounding heart and a shaky little smile, trembling with mingled doubt and desire. She was a fool in love, drawn by the magnet of physical attraction and daring to dream that this time he would give her so much more than a brief hour of happiness.

Patrick kissed her briefly, his mouth crushing hers with the promise of passion. Her hand fluttered and flew to his chest in swift, instinctive protest against the seeming lack of any love or tenderness in the way he took possession of her mouth.

He captured her hand, unsmiling. 'If you mean to go on fighting me, what the devil are you doing here?' he demanded, filling with a fierce dread that she would disappoint him yet again.

Sarah smiled ruefully. 'Don't give me

time to ask myself the same question,'
she warned. 'Or I might just change
my mind and go back to the dance.'

Instantly he turned off the ignition.
'Any doubts and there's an end to it!
Don't blow hot and cold with me,
Sarah! The time for those kind of
games is long past.'

His tone told her that this was her
very last chance. She sighed. 'This isn't
easy for me, Patrick,' she said quietly.
'I've been telling myself for weeks that
I don't want you.'

'Telling me, too . . . ' He didn't
look at her. The dark head was bowed
over the strong hands that gripped the
steering-wheel. 'Do you think it's easy
for me? My pride is just as stiff-necked
as yours. Do you know what it cost me
to swallow the things you threw at me
the other night and ask you to dance?'
It was a low, tense, reluctant admission
that he cared too much to dismiss her
from his mind and heart and life.

Sarah's heart turned over and her
hand seemed to move of its own

volition to stroke the crisp black curls and touch the lean, handsome cheek in a caress that was understanding and apology and love all in one package. 'I'm glad you did. Because I didn't mean any of them . . .'

He straightened and smiled into the eyes that were no longer flashing with angry, defiant fire, but glowed with a desire that was as fierce and as helpless as his own. 'I'm glad you said that . . .' Suddenly impatient to hold her again and thrill to the sweet seduction of her kiss and touch and lovely body, he reached to turn the ignition key in the slot. 'I don't know where you live. You'll have to direct me.'

She hesitated. Her flat was only a short drive from Hartlake but the minutes it took to reach it might be tense and strained. She was anxious to avoid another clash of proud and fiery temperaments and an abrupt cooling of the emotions that had brought them this far. Loving him, wanting him, eager to be in the arms that seemed so eager to hold her, she was terribly afraid that a wrong word or a wrong response might ruin everything.

'Could we go to your place?' she asked stiffly, slightly shy.

He nodded. 'Whatever you want.' He touched the hands that she'd locked into her lap, reassuring her, sensing and understanding the tangle of her thoughts and emotions. 'Trust me, Sarah. I promise I'll never hurt you again if I can help it.'

It was only a matter of moments before he brought the car to a halt outside the house in Clifton Street.

Sarah followed him up the stone steps to the heavy front door, trying not to think about Harriet Blake and the other girls that he'd brought to this flat in recent weeks. She couldn't afford to be sensitive about a sensual man's past, she told herself firmly. She could only hope with all her heart that she might prove to be the only woman in his life in the future . . .

14

The house was quiet, nearly dark. Most of its occupants were either on duty at the hospital or at the dance. Sarah's heart was hammering high in her throat as Patrick closed the door and ushered her before him into the living-room of his ground-floor flat.

'Make yourself at home,' he said lightly. He took the silk shawl from her shoulders, his hand resting for the briefest of moments, and then turned to lay it across a chair.

Sarah looked about her with very natural interest as he busied himself with bottles and glasses. It was very much a man's home, all leather furniture and plain carpet and drapes, expensive stereo equipment, rows of books lining one wall and several valuable prints and engravings. It had the stamp of his personality, she felt.

Strong and masculine and with an unmistakable air of quality.

She turned with a smile as he brought the drinks. He raised his own glass in a toast. 'To us,' he said quietly.

Her smile was suddenly tremulous. 'If you like . . . '

'And to Sir Henry.'

Surprise prompted a gurgle of laughter. 'Sir Henry!' she echoed, questioning. 'Why?'

'It's his night,' he explained. 'And if he hadn't decided to found a hospital we might never have met.' His dark eyes twinkled suddenly. 'I realise that I have yet to convince you that it was the best thing that ever happened, of course.'

'It was a long time ago,' she reminded him. 'I didn't have much reason to be pleased about it at the time, Patrick. When a girl gives her all she likes to feel that it's made some impression on a man's memory.'

He laid his hand along her cheek in a caress. 'I mean to make up to you for that,' he said quietly.

Suddenly shy of all that he actually promised with the warm tone and the look in his eyes, Sarah turned away from his touch. 'It's a nice flat. Very luxurious.'

'Friends tell me that it lacks a woman's touch.' Patrick drank the last of his whisky and put down the glass. He would have liked another but he had very good reason to stay as sober as possible that night.

'Do *you* think it needs a woman's touch?' she asked lightly.

'I know *I* do!' It was prompt, meaningful, and accompanied by a gleam of mischief in the dark eyes. He was surprised and delighted and moved to tenderness by the soft blush that dawned in her lovely face.

'That's the one thing you lack in your life, of course,' she teased, mocking him gently, doing her best to exorcise the ghosts who seemed to be haunting the place. Harriet Blake's distinctive voice was particularly loud in her memory's ear. She resumed her study of his books on their shelves, running a hand lightly over the spines, finding a few of her own favourites among them.

'You're the one thing that's been lacking in my life,' Patrick said quietly. He came up behind her and slid his arms about her like a lover, eager and trembling. Taken unawares, Sarah quivered to the brush of his hands across her breasts, the warm sigh of his breath as his lips lingered on the nape of her neck.

Desire was urgent in him, tensing the tall, lean frame, its throb finding instant echo in her own slender body. She leaned against him, loving him, thrilling to his need of her, the weakness of desire flooding through every vein.

His strong hands scooped about her small and tempting breasts, thumbs sweeping in slow caress over the buds that tautened beneath the thin silk of her frock. Sarah caught her breath on a shiver of delicious delight. Then she put her hands over his, pressing them to her, and turned slightly in his arms to meet the lips that were slowly trailing a route from her throat to her eager mouth.

His kiss seared her with the sudden fire of demanding passion. He murmured her name against her lips, rough with longing and growing intensity of need. On a sigh of surrender, Sarah turned fully into his embrace, sliding her arms up and about his neck, body melting in submission.

Patrick groaned and caught her to him so fiercely that her soft breasts were bruised by the crush. Then he lifted her and crossed the room with her in his arms to kick open a door that led into his bedroom.

Before he laid her on the wide, waiting bed, he looked into the lovely eyes that met his own so levelly, so unafraid. 'I'm not drunk this time, Sarah,' he said tautly, his voice harsh with the need to control the mounting tide of desire to ensure her satisfaction as well as his own. 'I'll make this a night that we shall both remember . . . !'

He was too quick with passion to be gentle in the way he undressed her, stripping the delicate silk frock from her slight body, the clever surgeon's hands that were so patient at their skilled and delicate work trembling almost too much to cope with infuriatingly intricate clasps.

Mature and experienced, he felt like a boy on the threshold of his first sexual encounter, and he was desperately afraid of disappointing her and himself. He was too near the edge of control. She was too lovely, too much loved.

He bent over her, kissed her eager lips and then slowly traced the lovely line of her neck to the hollow of her throat and the gentle slope of her shoulder and the soft, sweet curve of her breast. She put her arms about him and drew him down to lie beside her, to make slow, seductive love to her, to erase all the bitterness of the past with the sweetness of the present.

Sarah lay in his arms with the abandon of love and throbbing need while he burned her flesh with the heat of his ardent kisses and brought her to a fever pitch of arousal.

His lovemaking was more than merely expert. It was deeply caring, sensitive as well as sensual, swiftly perceptive as well as passionate, quickening her to new and unimagined heights of excitement and causing her to hover on the threshold of ecstasy, then slowing the tempo to extend her pleasure to limitless boundaries of delight.

Sarah had carried a dream of remembered magic in her mind and heart for years, but the reality far surpassed the romance. She felt that few lovers could know the kind of heaven that they were discovering in each other's arms, and she wanted to believe that the key to that heaven was a real and lasting and mutual love.

But she hesitated to speak of loving, although the words kept welling from

315

her heart to tremble on her lips. She could only transmit it through the way she kissed him, the many and instinctive ways that she caressed him for his delight, and the wholly generous and very sweet surrender of all she was and ever would be to the man she loved.

Recognising a change of urgency in his kiss, his sensual caress, the thrust of his body's need, her whole being seemed to expand with love and longing. She welcomed him, encompassed him, moved with him to the rhythm of quickening passion and almost swooned on the crescendo of the ultimate ecstasy. She cried out as the surging tumult of his powerful body carried her with him on the tidal wave of his triumph and the deep, dark waters of sexual fulfilment engulfed her completely.

Slowly, reluctantly, Sarah surfaced from that drowning in the sea of sensual delight, becoming aware of the weight of his body, the thud of his heart against her breast and the still of the lips that were resting on her own.

She put her hand to his dark head and stroked the fall of curls from his glistening brow with a tender touch. 'Patrick . . . ' She said his name softly, with love.

He stirred, just as reluctant as she had been to return to reality. He had made love to many women, but the touch and the taste and the sweet scent of Sarah, the supreme ecstasy that he'd never experienced with any other woman, had lingered through the years, haunting him with an elusive half-memory, filling him with an aching need that no one else had ever satisfied. It seemed incredible that he'd allowed her to slip through his hands all those years ago, even more incredible that he'd been lucky enough to find her again.

He was swamped with love and tenderness, a wave of emotion that transcended even the physical delight that he'd experienced in her warm and generous embrace.

'Sweet Sarah,' he murmured against her lips, thrusting his fingers through the gleaming mass of her hair that he'd loosened to cascade about her face and slender shoulders. 'I love you, Sister Sweet . . .'

He felt the quiver of a smile and the responsive flutter of her hand on his bare shoulder. He cradled her face in his hands. 'Did you hear me, beautiful dreamer? I love you . . .'

Sarah was still struggling with the shock of the first, totally unexpected declaration. She didn't know whether to believe him. She just didn't see that it could be true. Not when she'd been so horrid and cold and unapproachable all these weeks, never allowing him to get close enough to care for her as he claimed. She didn't dare to believe him. For didn't she have past experience of him as a man whose eyes and smile and warm velvet voice said all that a woman could want to hear, only to regret it before a new day dawned?

Her silence dismayed him. He sighed. 'Still doubting me, aren't you? Still judging me on my past record. What a hard woman you are! Sister Stone!' The warm tenderness of his tone took the sting from the epithet.

She turned into him, arms tightening about him, hearing the hurt behind the lightness of the words. But she couldn't express the terrible anxiety and apprehension that seized her heart. For would he still love her tomorrow . . . ?

* * *

Sarah's heart seemed to be beating uncomfortably fast as she pushed through the heavy glass doors into Main Hall. Even if her world had been turned upside down, her head and heart were full of Patrick and her body was still glowing with the remembrance of his lovemaking, there was still a ward full of sick people needing her attention. Love was no reason to neglect her work, she told herself firmly. But she wondered if she would be able to keep her thoughts and her feelings centred on the demands of her patients.

Jimmy was sitting at his desk as usual, big and florid and beaming. 'Good morning, Sister,' he sang out as she approached. 'Lovely day for it . . . !'

There was such a mischievous gleam in his blue eyes that Sarah was dismayed. Lovely day for *what*, she wondered as she hurried towards the lifts after bestowing one of her swift, sweet smiles on the all-knowing head porter.

She hoped that Hartlake wasn't buzzing with the news of her departure from Founders Ball with one of its most attractive surgeons. She didn't want everyone saying that she'd spent the night at his flat! She hadn't. He'd protested, but he'd taken her home at her request soon after midnight and she'd given him coffee. They'd talked and then he'd left her with a kiss and a hug that said much more than *he* was saying since she'd greeted his avowal of love with that hurtful silence. Whatever he felt, he wasn't committing himself any further, she'd realised — and she'd been grateful that he hadn't uttered any more impulsive words for him to regret this morning.

The lift that carried her up to the third floor was crowded. Sarah smiled and spoke in answer to two or three greetings from senior staff and was conscious of awed admiration and envy in the eyes of a first-year squeezed into a corner.

Had *she* been that youthful, that innocent, that awestruck by her seniors six years before? she wondered wryly. No wonder she'd regarded Patrick as little less than a god — idolised him as such and fallen at his feet in adoring submission when he deigned to notice her at last! She'd called it love and clung to that belief for a long time.

321

But she'd learned in the last few weeks what it really meant to love, deeply and irrevocably, and her education had been completed in Patrick's arms last night.

As always, her pulses quickened and her step became more eager as she walked along the wide corridor towards Mallory, her ward. But for once it wasn't the thought of the day's work and the patients whose welfare and well-being were her concern that set the adrenalin flowing, but the thought that soon she would see Patrick again. He was operating that day and she had two patients for his list on Mallory; he would follow his usual practice of visiting them before he went to change into surgical greens and scrub-up.

She was eager and excited and apprehensive all at the same time. Eager for the warm intimacy of a smile meant for her alone and excited by the memory of his lips and arms and urgent body — and afraid that overnight he would have changed his

322

mind about loving her, needing her, making her a lasting part of his life.

'Good morning, Sister . . . ' There was a little slyness in the smile of the night staff nurse as she looked up from the completion of her report.

'Good morning, Staff. What kind of a night have you had?' It wasn't Audrey Crane but a relief nurse. Audrey had managed to organise a night off to attend the dance and Sarah wondered if the girl had hoped to have Patrick as her escort when she'd made the arrangement. Instead, she had gone with a party of friends and danced with a variety of men and enjoyed herself in her usual light-hearted fashion. Sarah didn't have to feel guilty where she was concerned. She hadn't taken Patrick from the night staff nurse. She wasn't sure that she'd taken him from anybody. She didn't know that he was hers! She could only hope with all her anxious heart.

'Oh, quiet, Sister. The gods were kind for once in honour of Sir Henry.

I heard that the Ball was a fine success,' she added in her lilting Irish brogue and with a twinkle in her Irish eyes. 'And you went off with one of the prizes, is it right?'

Sarah laughed, colour swamping her face. Damn the grapevine and its occasional accuracy, she thought, knowing there was absolutely no point in denial. If it had reached the night staff nurse's ears then it must be all over the hospital!

'The gods were kind to me, too,' she agreed lightly, turning to hang her cloak in the cupboard and whisking out a clean apron. She fastened the wide black belt about her waist and smoothed the dark blue stuff of her sister's dress over her hips and tried not to remember the way that Patrick's hands had travelled over her wild-fired body.

She made her usual early-morning round of the ward, keen eyes observing every detail and sharp ears catching every sound, her sharpened perceptions aware of the juniors glancing and whispering and giggling in corners. The patients were almost as bad with their knowing smiles and sly glances and meaningful remarks that named no names but implied that they knew all about a ward sister's affair with a senior surgeon.

Sarah kept her cool with some difficulty, knowing that patients always brightened at any hint of sentiment in their clinical surroundings, remembering her own days as a junior and how she had thrilled to even the tiniest rumour of romance between members of the staff.

She just wasn't as sure as everyone else seemed to be that it *was* a romance, she thought wryly. She'd attracted Patrick's sensual nature. He'd made up his mind to get her into bed and he'd eventually succeeded because she couldn't help loving him. But his claim to love her might only have been prompted by the afterglow of their lovemaking, an already regretted voicing of a short-lived sentiment, not to be taken seriously or remembered in the light of day. She would know as soon as their eyes met that morning.

It was a moment that Sarah dreaded much more than she anticipated . . .

Mrs Spender clutched at her hand, the wrinkled old face wreathed in smiles. 'He's a lovely man, gel,' she said warmly, husky with sentiment. 'You hang on to him, treat him right, and he'll give you the world. Just like my Albert, he is . . . a good man. There ain't many of them, believe me. I've buried three husbands and only the first one was any good to me and I lost him too soon. Your Mr Egan reminds me of my Albert, he does . . . ' The rheumy eyes filled with the weak tears of the very old. 'Yes, you're a lucky gel and I'm very happy for you, Sister . . . '

Sarah patted the thin hand with a vague murmur of comfort. She didn't have the heart to disillusion the sentimental old soul. She wished she shared Mrs Spender's confident belief that her future lay with Patrick. *Your Mr Egan*, she echoed with a sigh of her heart. She would dearly love to believe that he *was* hers . . . for ever and always.

Leaving the old lady, she called her team of nurses into the office and listened with careful attention to the night staff nurse's report. Then, as the Irish girl went off to her well-earned rest, she organised the day's work, sent her nurses to do various jobs and began to be busy herself, doing her best not to watch the clock as the time drew near for Patrick's round.

She emerged from the clinical room as Harriet Blake thrust through the swing doors of the ward.

Sarah's heart sank at the prospect of a confrontation with the young house officer. She didn't like the girl, but she felt that she was certainly entitled to be annoyed that Patrick had taken her to Founder's Ball and ended the evening in the arms of another woman.

'Good morning, Miss Blake.' She

nodded with cool, careful courtesy.

'Congratulations, Sister! Hard work reaps its own reward, they say . . . and everyone knows just how hard you've worked to get what you want!' The girl threw the words at her, fury and disappointment edging them with malice.

Sarah stiffened, frowned. 'My ward is no place for a shouting-match, Miss Blake,' she said sternly. 'I won't permit you to disturb my patients with your tantrums. If you've anything of a personal nature to say to me then come along to my sitting-room and say it quietly.'

No one could be colder or more forbidding than Sister Sarah Sweet when she chose, as the juniors on her ward knew to their cost. But it was the first time that Harriet Blake had felt the full blast of her icy displeasure and it shrivelled her on the spot.

Having just heard what everyone else at Hartlake was discussing so avidly that morning, she'd rushed up to the ward to air her grievance. She was abruptly reminded that Sarah Sweet was *authority* and she was still just a house officer with her way to make in the world of surgery — and Patrick Egan was her boss and it wasn't wise to alienate him at this point in her career!

She swallowed her indignation. 'There's no point in saying anything,' she said sulkily, in low tones. She thrust her clenched hands into the pockets of her white coat, scowling. 'No man is a match for a determined woman.' She shrugged. 'Not that I blame you, I suppose. A girl has to use all her weapons to catch someone that attractive . . .'

She broke off as Patrick walked into the ward. He raised an eyebrow at her and she flushed and hurried away to busy herself with a patient.

The surgeon turned to Sarah, tall and broad and handsome in the formal dark suit and white coat, unruffled by the furore that he'd deliberately unleashed in the busy hospital. He looked at her without speaking, without smiling.

Sarah's heart sank as she looked in vain for a glimmer of a smile in those dark eyes. 'Good morning, Mr Egan,' she said stiffly, taking refuge in the formality that their surroundings provided.

'Do you suppose the foundations would collapse if you were to call me Patrick?' he asked pleasantly.

The drawling words and the sudden twinkle in his eyes lifted her heart just before it settled in her sensible black brogues.

'On the ward, Mr Egan!' she exclaimed, pretending shock and outrage, a smile coming and going with relief and thankfulness and the foolish desire to burst into most unseemly tears.

He sighed. 'Rules is rules, I suppose. But I think they might be stretched on special occasions. Like today. I'm sure Matron would turn a blind eye if I kissed you . . . ' He advanced towards her with an unmistakable light in his eyes.

Sarah backed away hastily. 'Patrick!' she warned. 'I mean . . . Mr Egan! Please behave yourself!' Alarm and admiration for his utter disregard for etiquette when it was a matter of proving his love were mingled together with the dismayed realisation that several of her nurses were craning their necks to observe the scene between sister and surgeon.

'One kiss,' he said firmly. 'To celebrate our engagement.' He put an arm about her and kissed her, warm and meaningfully, with love.

Sarah's heart was behaving most oddly. 'Our . . . our engagement,' she echoed blankly.

'Hasn't anyone told you?' He shook his head in amazement. 'I thought I could rely on the grapevine to spread the word. We're getting married, Sarah.'

'How do you know I want to marry you? How do you know if I love you or not?' Sarah's pride was fired by his sweeping assumption that she could want nothing more than to be his wife, although it was perfectly true, the one dream she cherished above all others.

'If you don't love me then you've no right to look so starry-eyed when I kiss you, Sister Sweet,' he told her sternly . . . and kissed her again.

It was against all the rules and the worst possible behaviour for a responsible ward sister, and no doubt the hospital foundations would start to crumble with the shock, but Sarah kissed him back with a great deal of love and a new confidence in the future that she would be sharing with the surgeon who'd been in such disgrace when he first came back into her life.

How could she not forgive and forget when she loved him so much . . .

WITH SOMEBODY ELSE
Theresa Charles

Rosamond sets off for Cornwall with Hugo to meet his family, blissfully unaware of the shocks in store for her.

A SUMMER FOR STRANGERS
Claire Hamilton

Because she had lost her job, her flat and she had no money, Tabitha agreed to pose as Adam's future wife although she believed the scheme to be deceitful and cruel.

VILLA OF SINGING WATER
Angela Petron

The disquieting incidents that occurred at the Vatican and the Colosseum did not trouble Jan at first, but then they became increasingly unpleasant and alarming.

DOCTOR NAPIER'S NURSE
Pauline Ash

When cousins Midge and Derry are entered as probationer nurses on the same day but at different hospitals they agree to exchange identities.

A GIRL LIKE JULIE
Louise Ellis

Caroline absolutely adored Hugh Barrington, but then Julie Crane came into their lives. Julie was the kind of girl who attracts men without even trying.

COUNTRY DOCTOR
Paula Lindsay

When Evan Richmond bought a practice in a remote country village he did not realise that a casual encounter would lead to the loss of his heart.

ENCORE
Helga Moray

Craig and Janet realise that their true happiness lies with each other, but it is only under traumatic circumstances that they can be reunited.

NICOLETTE
Ivy Preston

When Grant Alston came back into her life, Nicolette was faced with a dilemma. Should she follow the path of duty or the path of love?

THE GOLDEN PUMA
Margaret Way

Catherine's time was spent looking after her father's Queensland farm. But what life was there without David, who wasn't interested in her?

HOSPITAL BY THE LAKE
Anne Durham

Nurse Marguerite Ingleby was always ready to become personally involved with her patients, to the despair of Brian Field, the Senior Surgical Registrar, who loved her.

VALLEY OF CONFLICT
David Farrell

Isolated in a hostel in the French Alps, Ann Russell sees her fiancé being seduced by a young girl. Then comes the avalanche that imperils their lives.

NURSE'S CHOICE
Peggy Gaddis

A proposal of marriage from the incredibly handsome and wealthy Reagan was enough to upset any girl — and Brooke Martin was no exception.

A DANGEROUS MAN
Anne Goring

Photographer Polly Burton was on safari in Mombasa when she met enigmatic Leon Hammond. But unpredictability was the name of the game where Leon was concerned.

PRECIOUS INHERITANCE
Joan Moules

Karen's new life working for an authoress took her from Sussex to a foreign airstrip and a kidnapping; to a real life adventure as gripping as any in the books she typed.

VISION OF LOVE
Grace Richmond

When Kathy takes over the rundown country kennels she finds Alec Stinton, a local vet, very helpful. But their friendship arouses bitter jealousy and a tragedy seems inevitable.

CRUSADING NURSE
Jane Converse

It was handsome Dr. Corbett who opened Nurse Susan Leighton's eyes and who set her off on a lonely crusade against some powerful enemies and a shattering struggle against the man she loved.

WILD ENCHANTMENT
Christina Green

Rowan's agreeable new boss had a dream of creating a famous perfume using her precious Silverstar, but Rowan's plans were very different.

DESERT ROMANCE
Irene Ord

Sally agrees to take her sister Pam's place as La Chartreuse the dancer, but she finds out there is more to it than dyeing her hair red and looking like her sister.

HEART OF ICE
Marie Sidney

How was January to know that not only would the warmth of the Swiss people thaw out her frozen heart, but that she too would play her part in helping someone to live again?

LUCKY IN LOVE
Margaret Wood

Companion-secretary to wealthy gambler Laura Duxford, who lived in Monaco, seemed to Melanie a fabulous job. Especially as Melanie had already lost her heart to Laura's son, Julian.

NURSE TO PRINCESS JASMINE
Lilian Woodward

Nick's surgeon brother, Tom, performs an operation on an Arabian princess, and she invites Tom, Nick and his fiancé to Omander, where a web of deceit and intrigue closes about them.

THE WAYWARD HEART
Eileen Barry

Disaster-prone Katherine's nickname was "Kate Calamity", but her boss went too far with an outrageous proposal, which because of her latest disaster, she could not refuse.

FOUR WEEKS IN WINTER
Jane Donnelly

Tessa wasn't looking forward to meeting Paul Mellor again — she had made a fool of herself over him once before. But was Orme Jared's solution to her problem likely to be the right one?

SURGERY BY THE SEA
Sheila Douglas

Medical student Meg hadn't really wanted to go and work with a G.P. on the Welsh coast although the job had its compensations. But Owen Roberts was certainly not one of them!

HEAVEN IS HIGH
Anne Hampson

The new heir to the Manor of Marbeck had been found. But it was rather unfortunate that when he arrived unexpectedly he found an uninvited guest, complete with stetson and high boots.

LOVE WILL COME
Sarah Devon

June Baker's boss was not really her idea of her ideal man, but when she went from third typist to boss's secretary overnight she began to change her mind.

ESCAPE TO ROMANCE
Kay Winchester

Oliver and Jean first met on Swale Island. They were both trying to begin their lives afresh, but neither had bargained for complications from the past.

CASTLE IN THE SUN
Cora Mayne

Emma's invalid sister, Kym, needed a warm climate, and Emma jumped at the chance of a job on a Mediterranean island. But Emma soon finds that intrigues and hazards lurk on the sunlit isle.

BEWARE OF LOVE
Kay Winchester

Carol Brampton resumes her nursing career when her family is killed in a car accident. With Dr. Patrick Farrell she begins to pick up the pieces of her life, but is bitterly hurt when insinuations are made about her to Patrick.

DARLING REBEL
Sarah Devon

When Jason Farradale's secretary met with an accident, her glamorous stand-in was quite unable to deal with one problem in particular.

THE PRICE OF PARADISE
Jane Arbor

It was a shock to Fern to meet her estranged husband on an island in the middle of the Indian Ocean, but to discover that her father had engineered it puzzled Fern. What did he hope to achieve?

DOCTOR IN PLASTER
Lisa Cooper

When Dr. Scott Sutcliffe is injured, Nurse Caroline Hurst has to cope with a very demanding private case. But when she realises her exasperating patient has stolen her heart, how can Caroline possibly stay?

A TOUCH OF HONEY
Lucy Gillen

Before she took the job as secretary to author Robert Dean, Cadie had heard how charming he was, but that wasn't her first impression at all.

ROMANTIC LEGACY
Cora Mayne

As kennelmaid to the Armstrongs, Ann Brown, had no idea that she would become the central figure in a web of mystery and intrigue.

THE RELENTLESS TIDE
Jill Murray

Steve Palmer shared Nurse Marie Blane's love of the sea and small boats. Marie's other passion was her step-brother. But when danger threatened who should she turn to — her step-brother or the man who stirred emotions in her heart?

ROMANCE IN NORWAY
Cora Mayne

Nancy Crawford hopes that her visit to Norway will help her to start life again. She certainly finds many surprises there, including unexpected happiness.

No.	Date	No.	Date	No.	Date	No.	Date
1	10/02	25		49		73	
2	1/17	26		50		74	
3	7/00	27		51		75	
4	9/15	28		52	9/10	76	
5		29		53		77	
6	8/21	30		54		78	
7		31	6/10	55		79	12/19
8	9/03	32		56		80	
9		33		57		81	
10		34		58		82	8/19
11		35		59		83	
12		36		60		84	
13	2/18	37		61	4/14	85	
14	4/13	38		62		86	
15		39		63		87	
16		40		64		88	
17		41		65		89	
18		42		66		90	
19		43		67		91	
20		44		68		92	
21	9/18	45	2/12	69		COM	
22		46	12/10	70			
		47		71	10/14		
		48		72			

n't
one;
ams
took